From My Front Porch

From My Front Porch

LEIGH McKNIGHT

URBAN BOOKS
http://www.urbanbooks.net

This is a work of fiction. Any references or similarities to actual events, real people, living or dead, or to real locales are intended to give the novel a sense of reality. Any similarity in other names, characters, places, and incidents is entirely coincidental.

URBAN SOUL is published by

Urban Books
1199 Straight Path
West Babylon, NY 11704

Copyright © 2008 by Leigh McKnight

All rights reserved. No part of this book may be reproduced in any form or by any means without the prior written consent of the Publisher, excepting brief quotes used in reviews.

ISBN-13: 978-1-59983-043-8
ISBN-10: 1-59983-043-4

First Printing: August 2008

10 9 8 7 6 5 4 3 2 1

Printed in the United States of America

Chapter 1

"Ladies and gentlemen, we'll be landing shortly at La Guardia Airport," announced the pilot. "I hope you've enjoyed your flight on United Airlines. Have a great day."

Within minutes the plane touched down on the runway and cruised to a stop. Rayanne Wilson jumped up from her seat, reached into the overhead compartment, grabbed her carry-on, and was one of the first people off the plane. She strutted toward the airport, her stilettos tapping purposefully on the tarmac. Once inside the airport, she quickly made her way to the baggage claim area.

She glanced around, her silky hair falling over her shoulders, as she was mesmerized by the sights and sounds, by the enormous number of people leaving and arriving from cities all over the world. She grinned, absorbing the fact that she was in New York City. All her life she'd dreamed of leaving her sleepy South Carolina hometown for the glam and glitz of the Big Apple. She wanted to be rich and famous, and New York City called to her in a way no place else ever had. So there she was, twenty-two years old, armed with her degree and ready to make her dreams come true.

She searched the crowd for her best friend's familiar face. They spotted each other at the same time and rushed toward each other.

"Girl, I'm so glad you're here! How are you? How's everyone at home? Did you have a good flight?" Ivory's questions tumbled out in her excitement. "And look at you—you look like you could be a model rather than a budding playwright."

Rayanne hugged her friend, laughing at the sheer pleasure of being with her again. "You're the one who's gorgeous! Look at you—a real *Cosmo* girl."

Ivory's name was a stunning contrast to her appearance—model tall and model thin, her complexion flawless and black as coal. Her hair was dark brown and long and she wore it straight. But her face was her stock-in-trade. With her beautiful hazel eyes—framed by long dark lashes—pert nose, and pouty mouth, Ivory drew people's attention everywhere they went.

Ivory's laughter tinkled like champagne pouring over an ice sculpture as she and Rayanne made their way to the baggage carousel. "Dorian couldn't make it. She'll be at the loft when we get there. Dorian is the greatest. You're going to love her."

"After all that you've told me about her, I love her already," Rayanne said as the first pieces of luggage hit the conveyor belt.

"I just know we're going to have a blast." Ivory took the claim tickets from Rayanne. "Please tell me you don't still have that yucky orange set Mama Helen bought you eons ago. If you do, I can tell you right now—Dorian's going to throw it in the garbage. But, being the sweetheart she is, she'll buy you a new set."

Rayanne laughed. "My luggage is brown and new, thank you very much. Mama gave me a new set for graduation."

Ivory rolled her eyes, then compared the ticket numbers to the pieces Rayanne pointed out and pulled them from the carousel. "I'm impressed. Mama Helen's taste has vastly improved."

"Well, you're going to be *pressed* when I tell her what you said. You know you don't want to mess with my mama. She'll take you out like a bad bag of trash."

"Yeah, like she did that deadbeat Sunny P, who thought he was going to play you and every other girl in school."

They laughed again, gathering her luggage, as they reminisced about Mama Helen's escapades. Mama Helen's philosophy was simple: no one messed with her family unless they wanted to bear the brunt of her big, heavy salad spoon!

When they'd collected all the luggage, Ivory led the way to a waiting limo.

"Wow." Rayanne's gaze slid over the sleek black ride, which was sweet with its polished chrome accents. "Modeling must be paying very well."

"Heck no—I'm waitressing in between assignments." Ivory grinned. "This is courtesy of Dorian's significant other."

"Does he have any friends?" Rayanne asked as she got in and moved across to the other window, making room for Ivory. "Maybe a handsome brother?"

Within minutes they were gliding through New York City traffic, headed to the loft and Rayanne's new life. She stared out the window, her view filled with steel and glass skyscrapers, people, and limos and taxis. Even inside the plush car, she could feel the electric energy that was NYC. She and Ivory had made the leap from small town to big time. But it wasn't all that long ago when they were kids in school, excited about football games, cheerleading, and boys.

She and Ivory had been best friends since elementary school. They attended the same high school and college, and although Ivory was a year older and a grade ahead of Rayanne, they did everything together. Because they were two of the prettiest black girls in their school, they dated often. Sometimes they double-dated, but whatever they did, they'd had some hellacious times. They'd shared everything. Well, almost everything; Ivory also had a secretive side. Though she liked keeping people guessing, she never kept any secret more than a day. She liked games, and she was definitely a player.

There was a time when everyone in school suspected that one of them was dating Mr. Isaacs, the English teacher, but no one except Rayanne, Ivory, and Mr. Isaacs knew which one it was. Of course, it was Ivory. Mr. Isaacs had fallen in love with Ivory; you could tell by the look in his eyes whenever he looked at her. Men fell in love with Ivory by the droves. How could they not? Rayanne thought. She was beautiful and far more mature than most of the girls her own age. She was popular and smart, and she had a great sense of humor. She was tall, slender, and graceful, but she was also a prankster, a trait that had carried over into her adult life.

Mr. Isaacs hadn't pursued Ivory until she was in her senior year of high school. Two weeks before graduation, he secretly asked her to marry him. Ivory refused, and although Mr. Isaacs was heartbroken, Ivory hadn't concerned herself too much. She came to New York to make her own dreams a reality. She wanted culture, career, and city lights. Modeling was her passion and marriage was so far off the radar it wasn't even a blip. She was going to be a supermodel. And failure was not an option.

Rayanne understood because she was just as passionate about her own dreams and they didn't include South Carolina, marriage, and regrets of what might have been.

"Rayanne!"

Jarred from her thoughts, Rayanne looked over at Ivory.

"You haven't heard a word I've said."

"Sorry, I was daydreaming. What did you say?"

"Never mind. We're here. I can't wait for you to meet our mascot."

Mascot? Rayanne didn't even try to figure that one out.

The majestic tower that greeted Rayanne rose to the sky. If she didn't know better, she'd think it went all the way to heaven. When she and Ivory entered the loft, dragging in the bags, Rayanne's mouth dropped open. "This is awesome."

"Glad you like it, 'cause it's home, sister girl."

Home was an understatement. Ivory's descriptions hadn't even come close to the reality. Rayanne couldn't have imagined the luxury, the elegance . . . and the vast space. It was like a picture out of *Luxury Homes and Gardens* magazine.

The loft was a beautiful symphony of pink and white, airy and spacious with French doors that stood open to the terrace. As Ivory gave her the tour, Rayanne found there were living and dining rooms, a den, a full kitchen, a guest bathroom, three bedrooms with accompanying bathrooms, and a lovely terrace.

The oval cherry-wood table, set for six, sat in the middle of the dining room. A lush arrangement of pink silk flowers adorned the center of the table and two candles in crystal holders sat on either side of the arrangement. A magnificent crystal chandelier hung over the center of the table. Rayanne envisioned the many formal dinner parties they were going to hold in that gorgeous room.

The artwork adorning the walls of the loft blended perfectly with everything, and the plants gracing the rooms were the crowning touch. The walls and drapes were white, the windows were large and deep, and while some of the hardwood floors were polished and buffed until they shone, others were laid with exquisite replicas of priceless oriental rugs. The skylight, coupled with the windows, let in unlimited light. The terrace held a white painted wrought-iron table with matching chairs, and the white flower boxes housed real geraniums.

A promenade was built a couple of floors down and flowers, benches, people strolling, while others sat engrossed in conversations or just relaxing in the sun, were visible. A lawn, resembling plush green carpeting, ran almost the full length of the promenade. It was a place of beauty, and although Rayanne was in complete awe of her new home, the terrace with the view was the main attraction for her, not to mention the huge fish tank that held an assortment of tropical fish.

Rayanne could hardly believe she'd be living in a place like that, sharing such elegance.

"Dorian! We're here!" Ivory called out as they neared the bedrooms.

A jade-eyed blonde holding a cat rushed out of

one of the rooms. She set the cat on the floor and gave Rayanne a big hug.

"It's so good to finally meet you. I'm glad you're here. You're all Ivory ever talks about."

"All good things, I hope," Rayanne said with a smile.

Dorian had to be six feet tall, if an inch. "Absolutely. How was your flight?"

"It was fine, but I thought I'd never get here." Rayanne grinned. "I'm on a serious high. I've become a New Yorker."

Dorian and Ivory laughed. "Well, that takes care of introductions, except for Sapphire," Ivory said.

"Sapphire?" Rayanne was puzzled. Was there a fourth roommate?

"Our little mascot over there," Ivory said, pointing to the cat who was observing the girls. "She thinks she owns the place. The way she has taken over around here, she should be paying rent."

They all laughed.

"So that's our fourth roommate," Rayanne said.

"Yes, that's my baby," Dorian said. "She was a gift for my nineteenth birthday."

"She's precious," Rayanne said. The cat's eyes were like huge blue gems. It was obvious why Dorian had named her Sapphire.

"Yeah, precious Sapphire," Ivory said, pulling out a pack of cigarettes.

Rayanne saw Ivory light a cigarette. Ivory had told Rayanne that she wasn't the same little girl that left South Carolina, but how much had she changed? Rayanne wondered.

"When did you start smoking?" she asked, knowing how important good health was to them.

"A couple of months ago," Ivory replied, then

said to Dorian, "Didn't I tell you she can be an old mother hen?"

"Why would you want to smoke? It's so not healthy," Rayanne said, reaching for the cigarette.

Ivory quickly moved her hand out of reach. "I only do it occasionally."

"But those things will kill you," Rayanne said.

"If this doesn't kill me, something else will, so what's the difference?" Ivory teased.

"Smoking is a nasty habit, but if you don't care about your own health, be considerate of Dorian and me. Secondary smoke is just as dangerous," Rayanne replied.

"Yeah, yeah, yeah," Ivory said, and noticing the frown on Rayanne's forehead, she added, "And get that buckle out of your brow."

"You sound just like mama," Rayanne said.

"I know," Ivory said, and she turned to Dorian to explain. "When Rayanne would have something heavy on her mind, she always wrinkled up her forehead and her mother would say," Rayanne and Ivory said in unison, "'Honey, get that buckle out of your brow.'"

The girls laughed.

"Girl, I'm so glad you're here and I hope you'll like the place," Ivory said. "Dorian and I love it."

"What's not to like? This place blows my mind," Rayanne said, and she went on and on about the skyline, the huge city, and the crowds.

"You're so country," Ivory joked.

"Who are you calling country?" Rayanne asked. "We both come from the same small country town."

"You're still country," Ivory said with a grin. "I, on the other hand, have arrived. I'm an official city girl."

"Stop fighting and let's show Rayanne the skyline

from the balcony." Dorian didn't wait for a response but led the way to the terrace.

Rayanne and Ivory joined Dorian. Peering over the balcony, they viewed the city as Diana Ross's swan song to The Supremes, "Someday We'll Be Together," came from the oldies but goodies radio station playing in the loft. Even though the song was old, it still sounded good.

As the girls peered out over the balcony, Rayanne said, "This is great." Then looking from Ivory to Dorian, she said, "So the two of you met at a modeling agency."

"We both answered a call for a modeling assignment," Dorian said, leaning against the rail. "Ivory broke a nail and panicked when she couldn't find her repair kit. I don't know why, though. She had everything in that bag *and* the kitchen sink. So"—Dorian put a beautifully manicured hand to her chest—"*moi* stepped in and helped a sister out."

"You just want to be black so bad," Ivory said, then laughed.

"Which of you got the job?" Rayanne asked.

"Neither, but Dorian and I have been friends ever since."

"Dorian bought my friendship for the price of a tiny little nail," Ivory said, lifting up one finger and flashing a nail. "And that's a true story."

"That's a great story," Rayanne said. "Ivory talked about you all the time."

"Okay, okay, that's enough. Let's not give old big head over here the big head." Ivory ushered everyone back inside.

"Are you hungry?" Dorian asked, when they had returned to the living room.

"Of course she is," Ivory said. "I'm sure they only fed her rabbit food on the plane."

"I was too excited to eat. The only thing I could think about was getting here," Rayanne said.

"Ivory and I are going to take you out to dinner, but I can make up a sandwich or something for you now," Dorian offered.

"No, I'm fine. Thanks." Rayanne stood in the center of the living room. She slowly turned around, marveling at her fairy-tale surroundings. "Talk about atmosphere. This is magnificent. Trump Towers couldn't be any better than this."

Ivory shook her head and rolled her eyes. "What'd you expect—that I'd bring you to a dump?"

"Of course not." Rayanne spread her arms wide. "But I didn't expect this."

"Come see your room." Dorian gathered up Sapphire in her arms and led the way to Rayanne's room, which was the middle bedroom.

"Dorian fixed it up for you all by herself," Ivory said, following the two girls. "I told her your favorite color is yellow, and the woman went to work."

Rayanne's bedroom back home was very comfortable, but this room was spacious and elegant and it was a far cry from her old bedroom. The room and its accompanying bath were done in yellow and white. The bed was almost covered with pillows and the vanity was well stocked with toiletries.

Dorian's bedroom was pink and white and Ivory's was white, except for the mint-green dust ruffle on her bed.

Dorian and Ivory helped Rayanne bring her bags into her new room, and then they helped her put her clothes away and stored the empty luggage in the closet.

Rayanne brought Ivory up to date on what was happening back home; then Dorian and Ivory filled Rayanne in on some of their activities. Rayanne could tell that both girls were far more adventurous and sexually advanced than she, and although she wasn't without carnal knowledge of men, listening to them made her wonder if she'd been living under a rock all that time.

"So are we on for tonight?" Dorian asked.

"You know it," Ivory said, and it was settled.

The girls got dressed and took a taxi to a restaurant that adjoined to a nightclub. When they got to the door Rayanne was worried. "How are we going to get into a nightclub?" she asked. "None of us are twenty-one."

"Oh, girl, we've got the hookup," Ivory said.

She'd barely finished speaking when a tall, muscular hunk with a mega-sexy smile opened the door. "Hey, Ivory, good to see you tonight." He stood aside and they walked past him. Rayanne couldn't stop staring at him. She didn't think she'd ever seen a guy so fine.

"You say that to all the girls, A.C." Ivory gave him a saucy grin.

"Yeah, but I mean it when I say it to you." He nodded to Dorian. "What's up?" Then his gaze fell on Rayanne and her toes curled in her shoes. "Who's your new friend, Ivory?"

"Rayanne is my best friend from home. Get used to seeing her. She's just moved to the city and is living with Dorian and me."

"Nice meeting you, Rayanne." The way he said her name, sensuality dripping from his voice, made Rayanne do an old-fashioned swoon. Speech was beyond her, so she gave him a weak smile and followed Ivory and Dorian into the club. When they'd found a table, Ivory ordered soft drinks.

After the waiter left, Ivory turned to Rayanne. "Rule—never, ever date a bouncer. Ever. If the relationship goes sour, you'll never get in the club again—free or not."

"Word." Dorian's voice was somber as she confirmed rule number one. Rayanne had to laugh; it sounded so funny coming from Dorian's cultured voice.

"Ladies, I think we've found dinner."

Rayanne followed Ivory's gaze to a man sitting at the bar, close to their table. He couldn't seem to keep his eyes off Ivory. She smiled at him and ran her tongue slowly over her lips, and he melted like a peanut butter and jam sandwich in a toaster oven. And she'd noticed him as well. With a nod, she beckoned him over. He slid, nearly falling, off the bar stool in his haste to get to the table. Recovering his balance, he sucked in his gut, pushed his shoulders back, and swaggered over to their table. Rayanne couldn't believe her eyes as she watched him preen for Ivory.

"How are you, handsome?" Ivory's voice was low and seductive.

"Fine, beautiful." He was eating her up with his eyes. "How are you ladies this evening?"

He never took his eyes off Ivory, and Rayanne was glad. She was having the hardest time concealing her laughter. Dorian, however, was all into the game. She smiled with a sultry wink, when the stranger glanced at her. Rayanne never knew if he'd looked at her or not. If she'd looked up, she'd have howled with laughter. He looked old enough to be their father.

"Would you like to join us?" Ivory smiled at him.

"Sure." The man took a seat next to Ivory. "Are you ladies alone this evening?"

"We're alone most evenings," Ivory lied.

"I find that hard to believe," he said with a brief glance at Rayanne and Dorian. "Can I get you ladies anything?"

"Actually I haven't eaten since breakfast," Ivory said.

"Well, why don't we do something about that?" He got up from the table. "Why don't you and your friends join me for dinner? Whatever you want . . . however you want," he added with a grin. He probably thought it was sexy, but to Rayanne it looked as if he was in pain.

"Come on, ladies. This nice gentleman is treating us to dinner." Ivory, never missing a beat, linked her arm through his and let him lead her into the restaurant. As Dorian and Rayanne followed, she glanced over her shoulder and winked at them.

Dorian whispered to Rayanne, "She's done it again."

After they'd eaten all the scampi they could handle and drunk all the wine they wanted, Ivory announced that she was ready to go home. William Geter was visibly disappointed. He didn't object to treating the ladies to dinner; it seemed he had expected to get Ivory's phone number. Instead, they thanked Mr. Geter and said good night.

"Chances are he is somebody's daddy and should be at home with them instead of roaming around the streets looking for fresh meat anyway," Ivory said.

"Isn't she something?" Dorian said. "She has taken the poor guy for a ride and now she's talking smack about him. He was probably a nice guy."

"Who knows? But who gives a damn?" Ivory said.

"Girl, where did you learn to curse so?" Rayanne laughed.

They hailed a taxi and Ivory gave the address. When the taxi rolled to a stop in front of a nightclub, there were lines of people standing outside, waiting to get in. Rayanne knew they were at *the* place to party.

Everyone seemed to know Ivory and Dorian, especially the two fine, buff black men guarding the door. They were, obviously, the men to know since they decided who got in and who didn't. Thank goodness Ivory wouldn't have to pull one of her hustles to get them inside. Rayanne still felt bad about the restaurant incident—she should have paid for her own meal regardless of what Ivory or Dorian had done.

When the two bouncers saw the three of them weaving through the crowd, one of them said, "Ivory, Dorian, get on in here."

"Hey, Scorpio. What's up, DiAngelo?" Ivory said to them.

"Hey, guys," Dorian said.

"Wad up, ladies?" he said when they reached him.

"This is Rayanne," Ivory said and after the two men gave Rayanne some love, the girls went inside the club. Rayanne was surprised by the sheer number of people the club held. Bodies were packed everywhere. The music was loud but it didn't stop her from having the time of her life. She danced for hours, damp with perspiration, until Ivory and Dorian pulled her from the club.

"It's time to go home," Dorian said. "We got a lot to do tomorrow."

"I was having fun," Rayanne protested. Even though it was a warm evening, her damp dress was cold against her skin. "Do you guys party like that all the time?" she asked as Ivory hailed a taxi.

"Every chance we get," Dorian said. As a taxi stopped in front of them, Dorian shook her head. "I don't know how she does it."

"Does what?" Rayanne followed her friends into the cab.

"Get cabs. *All* the time. The girl's got a hundred percent record."

Rayanne rested her head on the back of the seat as they rode. Ivory seemed to have become accomplished at a lot of things. And not all of them good. Rayanne loved Ivory like a sister, but she was realizing the Ivory she had known in South Carolina was a far cry from the Ivory she was getting to know in New York City.

"Did you have a good time?" Ivory asked, looking over at Rayanne.

"Good with a capital 'G'," Rayanne replied. "That place was off the hook—and all those wall-to-wall brothers, each one finer than the next, a girl could become addicted."

"When I came to New York, I'd never seen so many good-looking men in my life," Ivory said. "Just when I thought I'd seen God's most perfect creation, I would look around and there would be another one who blew the other one out of the water."

"It's always like that," Dorian said.

"When are we going back there?" Rayanne asked.

Ivory and Dorian laughed. "Girlfriend is gonna love New York," Dorian said.

For a moment they rode in silence until Ivory said, "I don't have any more money." She looked at Rayanne. "Do you have any?"

"I've got—" Ivory elbowed Rayanne, and the pain

cut off her words. "N-no, I don't have any," Rayanne amended weakly.

"Me neither," Dorian said. "I spent my last twenty on the last round of drinks we had."

Rayanne stared at them. They hadn't spent a dime in the club. She had a sinking feeling in her stomach. She smelled another hustle.

"Er, driver," Ivory said, tapping the back of the driver's seat. "What happens if we don't have any money?"

He glanced up into the rearview mirror. "You don't have any money?"

"Well, we just realized none of us saved any money."

Rayanne saw his back stiffen. She glanced out the window wondering if they were about to get their butts beaten by their Puerto Rican driver.

"Lady, you know you can't ride for free." He glanced over his shoulder. "Do you have money or not?"

"I don't have a fucking dime," Ivory said. "We'll just have to owe you?"

Rayanne was shocked by Ivory's language.

"Owe me?" His laugh chilled Rayanne's blood. "You ride, you pay. No pay, no ride."

"Okay, okay, drive on. You'll get paid."

Rayanne exhaled the breath she'd been holding, glad Ivory had come to her senses. They rode on in silence, the driver watching them every so often in the rearview mirror. She wondered if he had a gun.

"Shit!" Ivory said. "You may as well pull over, mister, I'm as broke as a convict."

The taxi driver slammed his fist on the dashboard, jammed his foot on the brake, and the taxi skidded to a stop. "Get the fuck outta my cab," he ordered.

"You're going to put us out in the middle of nowhere? We don't—"

"*Now.*"

Rayanne didn't need to be told twice. She scrambled out of the cab, Ivory and Dorian quick on her heels. Their feet had barely hit the pavement before the cabbie gunned the engine and roared off down the street, the back passenger door flapping like a sheet in the wind. Ivory was laughing as the cab disappeared into the night.

"Have you lost your mind?" Rayanne was pissed. Ivory was obviously drunk to pull such a stunt. "You could have gotten yourself hurt—all of us hurt."

"Come on," Dorian said soothingly. "It was a harmless prank."

"Harmless?" Rayanne couldn't believe them. And Ivory was still laughing. "Shut up, Ivory. You may think it's funny, but I don't relish walking back to the loft in heels."

Ivory gave her a hug. "I'm sorry, Rayanne. It's the way people are here. Everyone's hustling someone. Anyway"—she squeezed Rayanne's shoulders—"we're only a block from the loft."

"What?" Rayanne stared at her. Ivory and Dorian looked at her face and burst into laughter again. "Yeah, right. Laugh at me if you want to. You wouldn't be laughing if that man had blown your ass into smithereens."

"You're right, Rayanne," Dorian said. "We shouldn't have done that."

"Yeah," Ivory agreed. "We'll be more careful in the future. Come on, let's go home."

Rayanne said nothing else, her heart pounding from their narrow escape. Ivory had pulled some tricks back home, but tonight's antics took the cake.

Rayanne was determined that in the future, she'd carry enough money to pay for her nights out. If she didn't have any, Ivory and Dorian could go out by themselves. She didn't plan on being a statistic in the daily newspaper. Period.

The following morning, Rayanne searched the kitchen for something for breakfast. Ivory and Dorian had gone jogging and hadn't yet returned by the time she got up. She opened the cabinets only to find a jar of instant coffee, a can of pink salmon, a can of tuna, and a large bag of low-sodium potato chips. When she checked the refrigerator, the results were no better: a container of strawberries, a couple of packages of cold cuts, a loaf of whole wheat bread, cantaloupes, a half quart of skim milk, and one shelf completely filled with bottles of water. Was that really the way models ate? Both Ivory and Dorian were thin as rails, and if that was the way they wanted to look, that was fine, Rayanne thought. But she wasn't a model, had no desire to be one, or look like one, and she certainly was going to have more than a bottle of spring water and a few strawberries for breakfast. Settling for a bowl of fresh fruit, toast, and coffee, Rayanne ate her Spartan breakfast, but resolved to have a nice southern-style breakfast tomorrow. After all, tomorrow was another day.

Rayanne had liked Dorian immediately. She found Dorian to be a wonderfully caring person, generous to a fault, and she was real down-to-earth, for a white girl. When Rayanne met Henry Farnsworth, the man Dorian was dating, she could easily understand his attraction for Dorian, but she couldn't understand Dorian's relationship with Henry—he was married. Henry was a well-dressed, clean-shaven older man, who owned a magazine company and major real estate, including the building that housed their wonderful loft, but he was still married. Despite his marital status, it was clear that Dorian wasn't going to give him up. Rayanne just didn't understand it. With all the single, available men, Dorian was crazy to get involved in a no-win relationship with Henry. However much it pained and disappointed her, Rayanne realized Dorian's love life was none of her business.

Rayanne also discovered that it was Dorian who bought food for the loft and anything else needed because Ivory's funds often ran short. It didn't take a rocket scientist to realize that, while Henry might have been good people, he was also Dorian's sugar daddy. Well, Rayanne thought, to each his own. She'd never become a kept woman herself, but she admired Dorian's business sense in choosing her "keeper." If you can't find love, find money, was what the old ladies used to tell her when she was growing up. Love could grow cold, but money could buy you a heater.

Rayanne found New York was exciting and there was always something to do, but with all the excitement and glamour, she still missed home and her family terribly. She found herself getting in constant touch with her parents, her sister, her aunt—even one of their neighbors and her mother's oldest and dearest friend. Just talking to them kept her grounded. She was often tempted to tell them of Ivory's pranks, but knew that if she did, her parents would have her on the next and fastest thing smoking back to South Carolina.

Shortly after her arrival in New York, Rayanne joined a small theater group. One day, after rehearsal, Rayanne was people-watching from the terrace. She had so much energy, as if something big and exciting was going to happen. She thought of Ivory's words that morning. Ivory had said they were two proud, strong black women who were going to change the world and leave their mark on everything they touched; and it was going to start there and then. They were going to make things happen. The conviction in Ivory's voice reminded Rayanne of the old Ivory she had known and loved. And even though the largest portion of Ivory's income came from waiting tables, Rayanne had no doubt Ivory would accomplish every goal she set.

Rayanne looked out over the city as far as her eyes could see. Like Ivory, she had her own passions and they were all about the theater: acting, writing, directing, or producing, it didn't matter which came first, just that they came. She knew it would take hard work, but she was no stranger to "sweat equity" as her father called it. She'd worked hard all her life; she wasn't about to stop now. She just knew that in New York, she could make her dreams come true. The possibilities and opportunities were endless. The city was large, it was frightening and if you weren't careful, it could be dangerous, but her destiny lay in the Big Apple and she was ready to eat it to the core. Right along with those delicious hot dogs Mr. Sal sold from his vendor's cart near the theater.

Chapter 2

Ivory and Dorian arranged their schedules to spend time with Rayanne and helped to familiarize her with parts of the city. Rayanne had brought her life's savings with her, including money she received as graduation gifts, which came to just over eight thousand dollars, but at the rate things were going, it wouldn't be long before she'd be out of funds.

The first couple of weeks, Rayanne met almost as many people as she'd known most of her life. She and the girls went to parties, movies, plays, and they danced many nights until they were soaked. They bowled, roller-skated, and enjoyed numerous other social functions, some of which required fancy evening dresses that they couldn't afford.

Rayanne laughed when she thought of the times when they were invited to functions requiring such a dress and didn't have the proper attire. It was Ivory who'd talked the girls into charging extravagant, gorgeous gowns, only to wear them, dry-clean them, if necessary, and return them. Rayanne chuckled even louder when once they went out and she'd danced, to Ivory's thinking, a little too much, and Ivory tapped her on the shoulder, telling her to sit her behind down before she soiled that dress and they'd have to have it for dinner the next two weeks.

One night after seeing a Knicks game, Rayanne, Ivory, and Dorian went to a basement party at one of Ivory's friends' homes. When they entered the basement, there was a large crown; some people were sitting around talking or having a drink, some were playing pool, and others were dancing. Rayanne, Dorian, and Ivory were on the dance floor almost immediately and when they returned to their seats, Ivory's dance partner accompanied her.

"What's up, Dorian?" he said.

"How is it going, Cal?" Dorian replied, with an unpleasant look on her face.

"Everything is everything," Cal said.

"Rayanne, this is Cal," Ivory introduced. "Cal, Rayanne."

"So you're Rayanne?" Cal said.

"I am afraid I am," Rayanne replied. "Nice to meet you, Cal."

"Same here. The girls have been taking good care of you?" he asked.

"Yes. They are great," Rayanne said.

"Good," Cal said to Rayanne, then to Ivory, "Can I talk to you a minute?"

Ivory and Cal excused themselves and Cal led Ivory across the room to the small bar.

"What was that look about when you saw Cal?" Rayanne asked Dorian.

"I just don't like the way he treats Ivory. He never takes her out and when they're together, he's always hitting her up for money," Dorian said.

Rayanne and Dorian looked in the direction of Ivory and Cal just in time to witness Ivory going into her purse and handing Cal a couple of bills, which apparently didn't satisfy him because she handed him another bill.

Ivory came back to join Rayanne and Dorian as Cal left the party with some other man.

"Ivory, what's going on with that guy?" Rayanne wanted to know.

"Cal? Who knows?" Ivory said and went back on the dance floor.

A few days later, Cal came to the loft. No one knew what Cal did for a living, but he was one gorgeous, chocolate brother and his brown bedroom eyes could easily suck someone right in.

Rayanne was in the kitchen when she heard Cal say, "I don't need a mother, Ivory. I just need you to help me out of a rough patch. Now, are you going to help me or not?"

"Cal, I'm gonna do it this time, but you can't keep coming to me for money. Besides, I didn't make that much in tips last week," Ivory said.

"When are you going to get a real job anyway?" he asked.

"Excuse me," Ivory said. "I don't see you out there trying to get any job. What's up with that? There are male waiters, you know."

"Whatever," he said, giving her attitude.

Ivory went to her room and returned with several bills that she handed to him and he left.

Rayanne came out of the kitchen.

"Ivory, wasn't that Cal and why were you giving him money again?" Rayanne asked.

"I just lent him a few dollars."

"Has he paid you back?" Rayanne asked.

Dorian came out of her room and joined them in the den.

"Who was that leaving?" she asked.

"Cal," Rayanne answered.

"Again?" Dorian asked.

"Since when do we care when one of us has a guest?" Ivory asked. "I don't say anything when Henry comes over."

"It not exactly the same thing now, is it?" Dorian looked sideways at Ivory.

"Well, actually it's not," Ivory said and Dorian knew she meant at least Cal wasn't married. "You should just mind your own business anyway." Ivory chuckled, as did Rayanne and Dorian.

Rayanne hadn't met Sean, but from what Ivory and Dorian told her, he was a nice guy. Why, then, wasn't Ivory spending more time with him? Rayanne thought.

Rayanne liked so much of what New York had to offer, even the church they attended. She'd soon become involved just as Ivory and Dorian had.

The weeks quickly changed into months, and as the season changed from summer to fall, not only was Cal coming by for money, but Rayanne's savings were rapidly being depleted. She had played all summer, but now it was time to establish some goals and work toward them.

Rayanne picked up the newspaper and began to read it. She saw that two people had gotten shot waiting for a train at the subway station. Another column listed the owner of a liquor store being robbed and killed. There were many other accounts of violence in the paper and Rayanne shook her head, wondering if the violence would ever end.

She examined the classified section, which she'd

done every day, looking for acting jobs. Unfortunately, the weeks that followed didn't even bring a phone call.

Just when she thought nothing would happen with her acting career, she got a call for an audition. She entered the loft to find Ivory sitting in the den, reading the newspaper, and Dorian doing homework.

"Girls, I have got a call to go to an audition in the morning," Rayanne announced.

"Really?" Ivory's face lit up. "You go, girl."

"Fantastic," Dorian said. "Good luck."

"Yeah," Ivory said. "Go knock 'em dead."

"Thanks, I'll try," Rayanne said.

After dinner, Rayanne said she was going to bed early. "I want to be well rested for my reading," she said.

Ivory looked up from the paper. "Night," she said.

"Good night, Rayanne," Dorian said.

Rayanne went off to bed early, but she was so excited about the audition that she wasn't able to fall asleep right away. Rayanne was the first to get up the next morning. She made coffee, showered, and dressed and left Ivory and Dorian having breakfast.

When she arrived at the room where the audition was being held, there were dozens of young women already there. After each name was called, some went into the private room and came out quickly while others stayed considerably longer. When it was Rayanne's turn, she was handed a script, given a little scenario, and told to begin. Rayanne read and when she was finished, she thought it went well; that is, until about one-tenth of the actresses were asked to stay while the others were thanked and told good luck. Unfortunately, Rayanne was with the latter group.

Rayanne was disappointed. She knew every line of that play and felt confident that she would at least be in the final consideration, but it didn't happen. On the way to work, Rayanne called Ivory and Dorian and shared her disappointment with them.

"It'll happen next time, sweetie," Dorian had said.

"We'll have some bubbly tonight," Ivory said, when Rayanne called her.

"Why? I didn't get the part," Rayanne said.

"And your point is?" Ivory said and hung up.

When Rayanne arrived home that evening, Dorian and Ivory were watching TV in the den and the dining table was set for three with candles lit and a bottle sitting in ice.

"What's going on?" Rayanne asked, halfheartedly, dropping her purse and newspaper on a chair.

"Did you hear about the rape that occurred near Central Park last night?" Ivory asked.

"Yeah. Everyone at work was talking about it," Rayanne replied.

"Not only was that poor girl raped, she was beaten badly," Dorian said.

"Sometimes I hate watching the news or reading the papers. You can't ever hear anything good," Ivory said.

"I know, I get so tired of the violence. It's so sad," Rayanne said.

"Rayanne, we are sorry you didn't get the part," Ivory said.

"But we have some dinner for you," Dorian said, sweetly. "So let's get started."

They sat at the dining table.

"We couldn't get the bubbly, but I hope wine will do." Ivory smiled and poured.

"Wine will do just fine," Rayanne said.

Since fall was coming to an end, Christmas would soon be approaching and Rayanne had very little money left. She had auditioned for two additional plays and each time she was sent away with a thank-you and good luck again. Although Rayanne had no plans for giving up on having a career in the arts, it was time to consider other possibilities to support herself.

She spent several days placing applications with temporary agencies, and almost immediately she received her first assignment. She was now a computer programmer at a bank. Working through temporary agencies was exactly what Rayanne wanted for now because that would allow her to go on auditions, with a simple phone call to her employer. Working at a bank wasn't her lifelong ambition, but the salary was decent and it helped pay the bills.

Shortly after Rayanne started work, she went to Central Park to have lunch. She stopped and got a hot dog and a soft drink from a street vendor. It was midday, the park was busy, and she felt safe sitting on a bench alone. She was reading a book and eating her hot dog when a stranger approached her.

"Mind if I join you?" he asked, holding a hot dog and a soft drink in his hands.

Rayanne looked up and met a pair of brown eyes and a nice smile. "I guess not," she said.

He sat beside her.

"I'm Lionel Walker."

"I'm Rayanne Wilson," she said, closing her book and placing it on the bench.

Rayanne told Lionel Walker about herself and learned that he was a junior executive in a recording company, he liked his job, he was single, and had no children. He explained that he'd been involved in landing several major artists for the company.

The time had passed quickly because when Rayanne looked at her watch, she had just enough time to freshen up and get back to work.

"Maybe we can do this again sometime," Lionel said.

"That would be nice," Rayanne said. They exchanged cell phone numbers and returned to their respective jobs.

Lionel called Rayanne that evening and they agreed to meet for lunch the following day, same time, same place. After having lunch twice in Central Park, Lionel convinced Rayanne to go to a restaurant with him for dinner one evening. Lionel liked gourmet food, fine wine, and good music and they went to a trendy restaurant and after they'd enjoyed a wonderful meal and more stimulating conversation, he saw Rayanne safely home. Rayanne enjoyed spending time with Lionel and they began going out regularly.

It wasn't long before Rayanne found she had a real affection for the city and an affinity for both Ivory and Dorian. And Lionel, the new man who'd come into her life, wasn't half bad either.

The movie the girls were watching ended at nine o'clock. Rayanne got up and turned off the TV set. "Good movie," Ivory said, and sighed.

Dorian sniffled. She removed several tissues from a box, wiped her eyes, and blew her nose. "Great movie. I always cry when I watch sad movies," she said and smiled. "Ivory always tells me that I cry at the sad movies, the happy movies, and the not so happy ones. She thinks that I just love to cry."

"It's true. When you saw *Imitation of Life*, you didn't pee for a week," Ivory joked.

"It was a great movie," Dorian said.

And it was true. Dorian especially loved old movies and she always cried while watching them. Everything old, according to Dorian, was sweet, and sad and romantic.

"Are we still going to the show at Radio City Music Hall tomorrow night?" Dorian asked, interrupting Rayanne's thoughts.

"Is that tomorrow night?" Rayanne asked.

Tweezing her eyebrows, Dorian looked up from the mirror she had sitting on her knees. "I think so," she said.

"Yeah, it's tomorrow night, but I'm not sure I can make it." Ivory smiled, resting her head against the back of the couch.

"You've got other plans?" Rayanne asked.

"I don't know yet, but I'm working on it," Ivory said.

Rayanne groaned. "When will you know?"

"I don't know that either," Ivory stated, and there was that secretive smile again, one that she'd reacquainted herself with recently. Ivory still got a kick out of keeping people guessing. She was usually very straightforward, but there were times when she could be just as mysterious.

Dorian said, "All right, out with it."

"It's no biggie. I'm just trying to decide whether I wanna go with y'all or do something else. Know what I mean?" Ivory replied, raising her eyebrows up and down in a comical gesture.

"You little hoochie. You have got something up your sleeve," Rayanne said. "And it ain't your arm."

"What's up with you? What're you doing tonight?" Ivory asked.

"I'm gonna call Mama, and return these books to the library. Afterward, I'm gonna stop by Lionel's for a minute. He wants my opinion on a CD of a new artist he's thinking about recruiting," Rayanne said, gathering several books from the desk and stacking them on the coffee table.

"Say hi to Mama Helen, and I love her," Dorian said and meant it. She hadn't met either Ivory or Rayanne's families yet, but she'd heard so much about Rayanne's mother that she looked forward to meeting her, especially.

"Say hey for me too," Ivory said.

"Y'all know Mama is going to talk to each of you before she hangs up," Rayanne said and dialed the number. "And I don't want you two staying on the phone all night. I want to get out of here before too late."

"Hey, Mama," Rayanne said, when her mother came on the line. "Yes, ma'am, we're fine. How are things at home? That's great. What's Daddy doing? Yeah, I figured he'd be busy, he's always busy. And Aunt Bessie and Mrs. Abigail?" Helen replied that Bessie and Abbie were as feisty as ever, especially Aunt Bessie, and Rayanne laughed. "Give Daddy and the others my love and I'll call soon."

When Rayanne was finished, each girl had a turn talking with Helen. Rayanne went into her bathroom to freshen up and was surprised when she returned with her purse to see Dorian still on the phone.

"What are you doing? Hang up that phone," Rayanne mouthed to Dorian.

After another moment, Dorian hung up. "Rayanne, I swear your mom is so cool," she said.

"She's something else. Mamas are so wise. I wonder whether we'll ever be as wise and together when we get married and become mothers," Rayanne said.

"Speak for yourself," Dorian said.

"Don't you want to get married and have children one day?" Rayanne asked.

"Sure. I want to get married, but children are kind of far into the future for me."

"If you intend to marry Henry and have his children, you'd better not put it off too long," Ivory said. "You're good to go for a few decades, but Henry, that boy is another story. He's just about ready for the old folks' home now." Sapphire made an entrance, stretched and yawned, and walked over to Dorian, who picked her up and stroked her.

"There you go with the age thing again," Dorian replied, but what she was thinking was that the last she'd heard it was still illegal to marry someone who was already married, and although she knew Henry loved her, he did seem to be dragging his feet on moving the divorce process along. But she said, holding Sapphire up and looking at her, "Isn't that right, baby? Talking about Daddy like that."

"I'm only speaking the truth," Ivory said.

"Dorian, are you going to finish your paper tonight?" Rayanne asked.

"I'm going to do interesting things like my nails and shampooing my hair," she replied.

"When are you going to do your paper?" Rayanne asked, knowing that paper was due soon.

"I have done the research already, and I'll probably write the paper tomorrow."

"When is it due?" Rayanne asked, walking over to Dorian.

"End of the week."

It was Monday night and Rayanne wondered, why wait? "Do you want to do it tonight?" Rayanne asked. "I'll be glad to help."

"Tomorrow is good. All I need is help organizing it."

"Okay, leave it on the table. I'll take a look at it when I get in tonight and we'll work on it tomorrow," Rayanne said, then looked at Ivory. "And what have you decided to do?"

"I think a friend may drop by, but in the meantime, I'm gonna do some laundry," Ivory said. "Anything you want washed?" She looked from Rayanne to Dorian.

"Yeah, that white blouse," Rayanne said, and dashed off to get it.

The girls didn't have any specific chores. Whoever was available did what was necessary and it worked out.

Rayanne returned and handed the blouse to Ivory.

"So, who's coming over? Sean?" Rayanne asked. She'd met Sean only once, but she agreed with Dorian, he seemed really nice. Unfortunately, Ivory didn't share their opinion.

"Sean?" Ivory said. "Get outta here."

"I thought Sean was history," Dorian said, setting a tray of nail care products on her lap.

"Sean is history," Ivory said, crinkling up her nose. "I quit seeing him weeks ago. You guys know how I love to kiss. Well, it takes some doing to get past his breath. I don't think that boy has ever heard of mouthwash."

Rayanne laughed. "You so crazy," she said, and asked, "Then who?"

"Cal," Ivory said, and poked out her tongue in a childish gesture.

"I can't believe you're still seeing that jerk," Rayanne said.

"What's wrong with Cal?" Ivory pretended to pout.

"What's right with him?" Rayanne asked.

Cal was the son of a New York police captain, but he was slick and cunning. She also knew that he was always hitting Ivory up for money, under the guise of it being a loan, only Rayanne believed that he never paid Ivory back. Ivory wasn't rolling in cash. She made good money with tips, but whenever Cal came around, most of the time Ivory was left unable to take care of her part of the expenses.

"Why would you want to waste your time with him?" Rayanne asked.

"That would be my question," Dorian said.

"Why? Why? Why? Why don't you two ask me something that is your business?" Ivory said.

"Ivory, you know Cal's a jerk. He has a colossal gall," Dorian said, filing away at a nail.

"You can say that again," Rayanne agreed. Cal wasn't one of her favorite people either.

"Cal's got it going on," Ivory said.

"Like what?" Dorian asked, lifting her hands to satisfy herself before applying the base coat of polish.

"Ivory, I get it that you have a thing for Cal. He's a good-looking brother, but he really is a jerk. That man, if we can call him that, has no scruples, so don't try to turn him into something he's not. Besides, you can do a lot better," Rayanne said.

"A heck of a lot better," Dorian agreed.

"Is there an echo in here?" Ivory asked, looking around the ceiling. "Of course I can do better. It's not like I'm planning to marry the guy."

Rayanne had a meditative expression on her face. She was remembering better times when she and Ivory dated guys who weren't nearly so self-centered, guys who were considerate and fun to be with. Unlike Cal, those guys had real working brains in their heads.

"Just be careful with him because a leach like that will take all the handouts you have to give and he'll never try to better himself," Rayanne said.

"Look, I'm a big girl. I can take care of myself," Ivory said confidently.

Rayanne had to admit it, Ivory had gone into relationships that were doomed from the beginning, but she'd always managed to land on her feet and she never got caught in the same situation twice. But still Rayanne wished Ivory would use better judgment in her relationships.

"This must be a class of men bashing," Ivory said.

"Just Cal bashing," Dorian said. "Cal's a smooth operator. So I'd pursue this with extreme caution, if I were you."

"You keep on and I will call Henry's woman, Olympia, on your ass," Ivory joked.

"Don't be sarcastic. We're just trying to help," Dorian replied, blowing on her nails.

"Save it, girls. I appreciate your concern, but I'm gonna go for it. I wanna see just where it leads," Ivory said.

"Why do you do things like that?" Dorian asked.

"Because she likes living on the edge," Rayanne said and grimaced at the thought of some of the situations Ivory had gotten not only herself into, but Rayanne as well, and the thought made her shudder. "She likes a good game. Whatever." Rayanne hunched her shoulders and looked at her watch. "Dorian, we'll work on that paper tomorrow. I'll see you guys later." She walked toward the door, turned, and looked over her shoulder. "Good night, Sapphire."

"We won't wait up for you," Ivory teased.

"I'm crushed," Rayanne said.

"Yeah, sure," Ivory said.

"Don't keep Lionel waiting," Dorian said.

"Go soak you head," Rayanne said, and as she opened the door to leave, the phone rang. "If that's for me, I'm not here."

"Don't do anything I wouldn't do," Ivory joked.

"Is there anything you wouldn't do?" Rayanne joked back.

"Not much," Ivory said.

"That's what I thought," Rayanne cooed at her, and laughed as she quickly ducked to escape the pillow Ivory tossed at her from the couch.

"I'll get your ass next time," Ivory said with a grin.

"Yeah, right." Rayanne laughed. "I'm not worried about you and your never-gonna-happen threats."

"Oh, I know you didn't go there with me, you nasty hoochie," Ivory said, but ended up laughing with Rayanne.

"It takes one," Rayanne said.

The phone continued ringing, finally interrupting their silliness. Ivory turned to Dorian. "Are you gonna get that?"

Dorian made a face, then picked up the phone. "Hello?" she said, and blew on her nails again. She looked at Rayanne and shook her head, mouthing that the call wasn't for Rayanne. Rayanne waved and closed the door behind her.

"Well," Ivory said, getting up from the couch. "I'm off to pull laundry detail."

"Knock yourself out," Dorian said to her, then

went back to her caller. It was Henry calling to say good night.

The following day, Rayanne and Dorian worked on her paper and Ivory went to be interviewed for a modeling assignment. But because of an inferior portfolio, she didn't get the job. Ivory realized at that moment the importance of having an up-to-date portfolio and she knew what she had to do. However, when results on Dorian's paper came back, she got an A.

As time passed, the girls became even closer. They held decent jobs, they dated frequently, but they always made time for each other, referring to themselves as the Manhattan Trio. They had dreams and goals, and they felt that together, they could do anything. They were unstoppable. If there was something they wanted and it was possible to obtain, they'd have it.

It was Rayanne's first winter in New York. She exited the subway station and walked toward the corner where the bank was. She closed her eyes and allowed the wind to hit her face. The air was frigid but she was dressed for it. That was another thing Helen had told Rayanne before she left South Carolina, and that was to have plenty of warm clothes, to bear a New York winter, was how Helen put it. Standing there in the freezing temperature, Rayanne realized once again that her mother was right and she had to agree, there was nothing as cold as New York in winter.

The three girls spent weeks tracking down the perfect gifts for their families, their friends, and each other. They watched as the tree was lit at Rockefeller

Center, and afterward they saw the Knicks play their last home game for the year. Three days before Christmas, after arranging with a downstairs neighbor to take care of Sapphire and the fish, they flew to South Carolina for the holidays. They alternated, spending nights at either Ivory's or Rayanne's parents' homes. Dorian met everyone, relatives and friends of both girls, and she was welcomed by all.

On Christmas Eve, they attended the evening services at church with their families and assisted Helen in handing out an assortment of presents to the children, and seeing the look on their faces was the best gift of all.

On Christmas morning, Rayanne got up early and went to her parents' room. She gently knocked on the door. "Come in," her mother responded.

"Good morning," Rayanne said and kissed each parent before sitting on the side of the bed, her mother sliding her feet over to make room for her.

"How you doing?" Helen asked. "You look good. Doesn't she, Raymond? New York agrees with you."

"It's big," Rayanne said.

"Is that all?" Raymond teased.

"No, Daddy, it's a lot more than that. It has so much to offer. I like it a lot."

"You still auditioning, honey?" Helen asked.

"Every chance I get. Nothing's happened yet, though," Rayanne said.

"Give it some time and trust in the Lord. It'll happen for you," Helen said. "Apart from the Lord, you can't do a thing."

Helen was a woman of deep faith and was always quoting the Bible.

"Always remember, girl, Rome wasn't built in a day," Raymond said.

"I'll remember that, Daddy," Rayanne said.

She never forgot to count her blessings. How fortunate and blessed she was to have the love and support from this incredible family.

The house quickly filled up with children that morning with Rayanne's nieces and nephews mostly. Some of them lived in town while others came from away to visit for the holidays, but the others were neighborhood kids.

When Maxine came in, it was obvious how much she and Rayanne missed each other.

Maxine was a few years older than Rayanne, but younger than their oldest sister, Lila, who lived in New York also. Maxine lived at home with her husband and children.

"What's going on, girl?" Maxine said, embracing her sister.

"Things are good," Rayanne replied. "What about you?"

"I'm fine."

"It's only been six months since I saw the kids, but they've gotten so big," Rayanne said.

"Don't I know it?" Maxine replied, then said, "I really like Dorian."

"So do I. She is great," Rayanne said. "Girl, I've missed you."

"Me too. I ain't got nobody to talk to now. You know there are some things that I can't talk to Mama about."

"Mama seems to know everything anyway," Rayanne said, and they laughed.

"So, are you seeing anyone?"

"Sort of," Rayanne replied. "Lionel is a friend. He's nice and smart and he knows what he wants, but there is no real chemistry."

"It's like that sometimes. The ones we want act like butt holes, but some of the nice guys just don't have that certain thing, you know," Maxine said.

The two sisters sat with cups of coffee and caught up.

Dorian was sitting on the floor with her legs tucked under her body and all the children sat on the floor in a semicircle around her and listened as she read to them. Dorian read with such expression that not only did the children hang on her every word, but some of the adults did as well, and when she finished the fourth book, the children begged for more, and she gladly obliged.

Ivory and Aunt Bessie arrived at the same time. Rayanne hugged her and after Aunt Bessie joined Helen and Raymond in the den, it was only minutes before the house became chaotic. Ivory got everyone involved in playing games. Some participated in karaoke and the house was filled with sounds of music, laughter, squealing children, and wonderful odors of food being prepared in the kitchen.

When Rayanne's two brothers and their wives came in, there was the exchanging of Christmas gifts. In addition, there was a gift from the family for Rayanne, Dorian, and Ivory; then they had dinner. Afterward, the kids went off and did whatever kids do, the men settled in front of the TV set for a game, and the women put away leftover food and chatted in the kitchen.

Dorian loved the closeness of the families, and although Rayanne thought she saw a brief touch of sadness in her eyes, by the end of the day, not only had Dorian been a hit with the children, but she had become an honorary family member, and Rayanne couldn't remember seeing her happier.

Rayanne received several phone calls, she placed others, and that night they joined friends, and from the time they entered the club, their table was frequented by all kinds of men, skinny ones, fat ones, short ones, tall ones, some were handsome, some not so handsome, but they all seemed to be there to party.

Lenny Clyburn, an old friend of Rayanne and Ivory's, sat at the table and the one thing they remembered most about him was how greedy he was while in high school. He'd sat and talked with them for hours, but not once did he offer them a drink, or anything.

Ivory removed a small box from her purse. She tossed one of the square white tablets into her mouth and dropped the box on the table. For something as insignificant as a piece of gum, Lenny's eyes lit up and became glued to the box.

Rayanne took two white squares from the box, popped them into her mouth, and placed the box back on the table. Lenny picked up the box and after he shook four pieces into his hand, he looked at Ivory and asked, "Do you mind?"

"Of course not," she replied. "Help yourself."

Lenny tossed the gum into his mouth. After a few minutes, he removed that wad of gum from his mouth and stuck it to the ashtray on the table. He shook out three additional pieces. He threw one more piece into his mouth and slid the other two pieces into his pocket.

"I'll hold on to these for later," he said.

"I heard that." Rayanne smiled.

"Lenny Clyburn, you haven't changed a bit," Ivory said. "You still look good, man. You were fine in high school, and you're still fine."

A part of what Ivory said was true. Lenny was tall, dark, and was even better looking now than when he was in high school, but what Ivory really meant was that he'd not grown out of his old stingy and greedy ways, and the man still didn't know how to treat women. He always acted as though women owed him something.

"You think so, huh?" Lenny said. "You are finer than ever yourself, sista."

"So, what are you doing now, Lenny?" Ivory asked, but knowing him as she did, it wasn't anything that would allow him to get his hands dirty or cause him to work up a sweat.

"I'm an insurance salesman," he answered, looking really pleased.

"Really? What type of insurance do you sell?" Dorian asked.

"Life insurance. Are you ladies well covered?" he asked, eyeing each girl.

"Does one ever have enough insurance?" Rayanne asked.

"Good question, Rayanne, and the answer is no," Lenny said over the music.

"I think I have as much as I need for the time being," Ivory said, and asked, "Where are you? Did someone say you're in Philly?"

"Yeah. Almost two years now."

"How do you like selling insurance?" Rayanne asked.

"It's not bad. It gets me out of the office several days a week." He grinned.

"Bet you get a lot of personal stuff done on office time. I know you, Lenny," Ivory teased, but she also knew that Lenny always got over any way that he could.

"Don't get me wrong," he began, "I sell a lot of policies. I made salesman of the month three months consecutively this year," he boasted.

"That's wonderful," Dorian commented.

"Yeah, congratulations," Rayanne said.

Lenny was a charmer and Rayanne and Ivory knew he'd used his charm to sell as many policies as he could to vulnerable women, whether they could afford them or not. Some of those women probably couldn't feed their families. As long as Lenny took home the almighty dollar, he didn't care about the consequences the rest of the world might have to suffer.

Lenny picked up the pack of cigarettes that Ivory had laid on the table, took out one.

"May I?" he asked.

"Of course," Ivory consented.

"That guy's a freaking moocher," Dorian whispered to Rayanne.

"He's always been that way," Rayanne whispered back.

"It's a good living," Lenny was saying. "I make good money, and I like what I do."

"It doesn't get much better than that," Ivory said.

"So, what are you girls into?" he asked, taking the gum out of his mouth, looking at it with a scowl on his face, and sticking that wad to the ashtray as well.

Ivory had a particular aversion to gum plastered in ashtrays, and the fact that Lenny put it there, put out his cigarette on it. and took another from her pack, was particularly annoying to her.

"I pick up a modeling assignment every now and again, but my main source of income comes from waiting tables," Ivory informed him. "Eventually, I plan to go back to school for my master's."

"Sounds good to me," Lenny said.

"Rayanne's a computer programmer at a bank, but she wants to act. She writes a little too," Ivory shared.

"You still writing, girl?" Lenny said to Rayanne.

"A little," she replied.

"That's great. I remember those plays you wrote while in high school. Some of them were pretty good too," he complimented.

"Thanks," Rayanne said.

"Yeah, she's still at it," Ivory said. "And Dorian is a graduate of New York University. She also models a little and waits tables, but she wants to own a modeling agency or perhaps a boutique shop."

Rayanne shared with Lenny the story about Dorian's waiting tables because Ivory did.

They chuckled and Lenny said, "You can't beat that kind of friendship, and in the meantime, you're waiting for that big break, huh? I hear ya. You sistas got it going on."

Rayanne and Ivory were thinking that Dorian certainly wasn't waiting for her big break. She'd found it when she found Henry, but Ivory said, "We're making ends meet."

Dorian took two draws from the cigarette she'd lit and put it out. She was trying to quit smoking. She reached for the box of gum, but Rayanne nudged her gently. Dorian looked at Rayanne and the eye contact alone told her that the contents of that box were forbidden. She looked at Ivory, who returned the look with raised eyebrows and a slight lifting of the shoulders, but the gesture was confirmation, and at that, a small snicker escaped Dorian's lips. Lenny didn't seem to notice the unspoken exchange between the girls.

As the night wore on, the girls prepared to leave,

but Lenny, prior to departing, noticed the box of gum still lying on the table. He dumped several more tablets into his hand and tossed them into his mouth. He handed the box to Ivory.

"You keep them," she said. "But save some for tomorrow." He emptied the box, tossed the last two pieces into his mouth, and they left the club.

"I hope Lenny hadn't planned a busy day tomorrow," Ivory laughed as she drove home.

"I know because when that laxative kicks in, he'll be out of commission for some time," Rayanne said and more laughter ensued.

"His behind is gonna be sore for a while," Ivory giggled.

"Rayanne, didn't you have some of the tablets?" Dorian asked.

"Yes, I had two pieces because I needed it," Rayanne replied.

"Oooh, I see," Dorian laughed. "Lenny is going to have one hell of a day tomorrow." They laughed some more.

"That'll teach him to use up all my shit." Ivory poked out her lips, pretending to be angry, but the squeals from the others made her laugh also. She laughed so hard that her head nearly touched the steering wheel.

"You'd better look where we're going," Rayanne laughed.

The girls didn't hear any more from Lenny that trip, and on December 27, after saying good-bye to their families, Aunt Bessie, Mrs. Abigail, and a few others, they returned to New York. But on December 28, the three of them boarded a flight for four fun-filled days in sunny California.

They checked into an economy hotel, rented a

car, and took in the sights, which included the wine country, the Golden Gate Bridge, and the rugged coast. They played volleyball on the beach by day and partied at night. When they boarded the plane for New York, Rayanne was quiet. She'd overspent and was worrying about how she was going to make ends meet until she got her next paycheck.

Rayanne had allowed Ivory to talk her into taking the trip to California, which she knew she couldn't afford, and although they had a great time, that trip had pretty much left her in dire straits. She'd not saved her share of the expenses for the coming month and was now wondering what she could do without over the next couple of weeks to free up enough money to meet her share of the responsibilities at the loft.

Rayanne looked over at Ivory, who was in the same financial situation, but didn't appear to be bothered by it. Ivory appeared not to have a care in the world, except when the next party was going to be. Ivory lived by the rule "live for today and tomorrow will take care of itself."

Rayanne was sitting in an aisle seat, with Dorian in the center, and Ivory at the window. Rayanne shifted her position and looked out the window on the other side of the plane. *God, please let me find a way to get over this hurdle,* she said to herself. *I sure hope I get an acting job soon,* she thought. Not only would it mean that she'd be involved in the kind of work she loved, but it would also put extra money in her pocket.

"You're quiet," Ivory said, interrupting her thoughts. "What's up?"

"Oh, nothing really. I was just thinking," she said, but what she meant was that she was worrying. The rent was one thing. Since Henry owned the property, he didn't mind waiting until the funds were available, but food, now, that was another story. It was Rayanne's week to shop for groceries and she had already maxed out two newly acquired credit cards. Thank God, those creditors had the foresight to extend a low line of credit. Otherwise, well, she didn't even want to think about that.

"What are you thinking about?" Ivory asked. "You enjoyed yourself, didn't you?"

"Yeah, I had a great time."

"Then what are you worrying about?"

"I didn't say I was worrying."

"You didn't have to say it, but I know you. You're worrying about the money you spent."

"That's a part of it," Rayanne said sullenly.

"What's the other part?"

Rayanne didn't say anything. Instead she just closed her eyes and let out a deep sigh.

"What's the other part?" Ivory repeated.

"Ivory, I am an adult and I have got to stop behaving so irresponsibly. I knew I couldn't afford this trip, but I went anyway. Now I am in a bind and I refuse to go to my family and have them bail me out. Mama and Daddy brought us up to be independent and they taught us to always be true to ourselves, and to not try to live beyond our means."

"Look, Rayanne, six months ago you graduated from college with honors. That was no small feat. You came to New York and shortly afterward, you went to work. You took a little time for yourself during the holidays before going back to work. You had a chance to relax a little and had a good time. Don't punish yourself for that."

When Rayanne didn't respond, Ivory continued.

"Hell, if we have to, we'll eat saltine crackers and drink water until we earn enough money to do better. I don't give a good damn. As long as we're together, we're gonna be all right, Rayanne, so don't worry, okay?"

"Okay," Rayanne said, but she wasn't convinced.

"Look, my friend, what's the worst that can happen? What are your creditors gonna do? Put a little blemish on your credit report, so fucking what? It's not like you got a car that they can come and repossess at night when you're sleeping. They'll get their money. Hell, so don't worry."

Rayanne looked at Ivory and smiled. "That's the idea," Ivory said. "Laugh about this crap. Soon you're gonna be so damn rich that these creditors will be licking your ass trying to give you credit."

"Good grief, Ivory." Rayanne couldn't help laughing. "You have a way with words."

Ivory laughed too. "All I'm saying is that tomorrow will take care of itself."

Rayanne thought about what Ivory had said and she agreed. There was no need to worry about her current situation because at the moment, there was nothing she could do to change it. She'd just have to let it go for today and see what tomorrow would bring. Then she changed the subject.

"It would be great if I got a call to audition for the play that is currently running at the Lester Theater. The original is going on the road, but they are recasting the roles and will keep it running in New York as long as possible," she said.

"Yeah. You could play any part in that play. You know all the lines."

"I always know every part for every play that I

auditioned for and I think the reading goes well, but they keep turning me down and that sucks."

Ivory tried to console Rayanne. "They're not turning you down. They just picked someone else for the project."

"They have done the exact same thing on all five plays I read for," Rayanne said, sulking. "I so want to do this one, though. This is a dream role."

Dorian had been asleep from the time they boarded the plane. She woke up, touched the corners of her eyes with her fingertips, and put her seat in the upright position. She stood up, tossed the pillow in the overhead compartment, and sat back down. "What going on?" she asked.

"We were talking about Rayanne's acting career," Ivory informed her.

"What acting career?" Rayanne said.

She knew she'd make it as an actress, but the real question was, when? How long would it take to get there?

"I can pick up a catalog ad or a local show when someone bows out for some reason or another, but nothing big is happening for me either, though I know it will," Ivory said. "You all know I went in just two week ago for a simple department store assignment and they didn't hire me because I didn't have a decent portfolio."

"I know it's gonna happen, but I get passed over so much that sometimes I get a little anxious," Rayanne said.

"There's nothing wrong with feeling that way. I feel that way sometimes also. I was so pissed off when I lost that photo shoot that was being done in London last month. It was the job to die for. I know we have to pay our dues, but I also know what I want, and I don't want to wait a hundred years to get it. I want it all just like that." Ivory snapped her fingers. "I've missed so many great opportunities because of not having a current portfolio. I want to tour the world, wear fabulous clothes, and strut my stuff up and down those long runways looking absolutely gorgeous, and I want to see this face on the cover of every major magazine in the U.S.A. and abroad. Yes. That's exactly what I want and I can't wait to have it."

Rayanne reached across Dorian to give Ivory five.

"And when that gig is over, I'm gonna decorate big beautiful homes for real families to live in," Ivory said. "But first things first. Portfolio now, decorating houses later."

"How is the portfolio coming?" Rayanne asked.

"I'm putting a little money aside for a photo shoot, so hopefully it will be soon."

"Ivory, I told you I will loan you the money," Dorian offered.

Unlike Ivory, Dorian already had an impressive portfolio and had gotten many lucrative assignments because of it.

"Haven't I told you I don't want you giving me Henry's money?" Ivory replied.

"Henry isn't loaning you the money, I am," Dorian said.

"Yeah, right. The money would come out of Henry's pocket to you, then to me," Ivory said.

"But you'd be paying it back," Rayanne said. "I think that's generous of Dorian to offer."

"It's Henry's money she's being generous with," Ivory said.

"Not so," Dorian said.

"Is too," Ivory came back.

"Not so," Dorian repeated.

"Play nice, girls," Rayanne teased.

Ivory lifted her hands in the air, settled back in her seat, and looked at her watch. "We should be getting home soon."

When the girls arrived at the loft, they checked messages and the mail.

Suddenly, Rayanne was heard screaming from her room. Ivory and Dorian rushed to see what was wrong.

"I got a call for an audition for the play I was talking about," Rayanne said excitedly.

Was her dream about to come true? Well, she'd know soon enough because she would return that call first thing in the morning.

That wasn't the only surprise they were in for that evening because shortly afterward, the doorbell rang. Ivory went to the door and answered it.

"Aaron," she said, swinging the door open.

It was the deliveryman from one of the neighborhood grocery stores.

"I have a delivery for you all," he said and proceeded to cart in the groceries.

The girls gave each other the high five. They knew that the delivery was due to further generosity from Henry. He was good about doing things like that, especially when he thought the girls might be a little low on funds.

When Aaron was about to leave, Rayanne tried to give him a couple of dollars.

"Thanks, but that's been taken care of," Aaron said.

The girls thanked him and he left. Rayanne knew that Henry's generosity couldn't have come at a better time and she was grateful. She also knew that Ivory was right again because tomorrow was already taking care of itself. Rayanne looked up at the ceiling and whispered, "Thank you, Lord, and you too, Henry."

Early on Monday morning, Rayanne made the call about the audition and on Tuesday, after ending one assignment and a promise to call for another in a day or two, Rayanne went for the audition. The part she read for was small, but two days later after waiting on pins and needles, she was called back for a second reading. She got a part. It wasn't the part she initially wanted, but she would be acting.

One play led to another, but the parts were small and didn't pay very much so she continued to work at the bank. Rayanne had charged so much on her credit cards that she was finding it difficult to keep her payments current. She kept up her expenses at the loft, but paying only the minimum on her credit cards wasn't getting her anywhere.

Eventually, Rayanne got the lead in a play, but it wasn't until she'd acted in several plays that she realized that she didn't feel the satisfaction that one should feel playing the lead in a play. She couldn't really identify with the characters she portrayed and as a result, she didn't feel she did her best work. Then it occurred to Rayanne that she'd rather create the characters she portrayed. When she was growing up, she used to make up stories and tell her family and friends, and because of her wonderfully creative and imaginary abilities, she was encouraged to pursue a career as a writer. Rayanne wrote and directed skits for her class while in high school as well as for other classes. She wrote poems for herself and her friends. Rayanne often wrote holiday plays and songs for her church as well as played the piano for the events.

When Rayanne decided that writing was what she wanted to do, she felt a sense of peace. The only problem was that to be a writer, she needed a computer. That was the first time Rayanne regretted running through the money she had when she came to New York, because now she'd either have to save to get that computer or pay at least one credit card down enough to get it.

Rayanne went out and bought a half dozen notebooks and she began putting her thoughts on paper by longhand. She came alive when she began writing. She enjoyed it so much that everything else became secondary and her career as an actress was short-lived.

When her phone rang that night, it was Lionel.

"Hey, Lionel."

"Why don't you come over for a while? I've got a nice bottle of wine around here somewhere," he teased.

"I'm sorry, but I can't tonight, Lionel."

"Why, what's going on?"

"I'm writing a little."

"Don't make me spend the entire night by myself," he coaxed. "You can get back to your characters later."

"Not tonight. Maybe later during the week."

"Okay, I'll speak at you later," he said and hung up.

Lionel was a nice guy and Rayanne liked hanging out with him, but she wasn't interested in getting into a serious relationship as he'd said he wanted. Before long, she knew she'd have to tell him how she felt. That was the only fair thing to do.

Chapter 3

"Sure you won't change your mind and come with us?" Ivory asked Rayanne one evening as she and Dorian were preparing to go out.

"I'm sure," Rayanne replied from behind her computer, her fingers racing over the keyboard. "I want to get this script finished and copied so that I can get it in the mail tomorrow."

"You never go out with us anymore," Dorian said.

"That's not true," Rayanne said, continuing to type. "I just can't go tonight."

But Dorian was right. Rayanne didn't go out with them or anyone else. When she began to write, everything else was put on the back burner. Romance and good times would just have to wait. She had goals and she wouldn't lose sight of them.

"You're always so in control," Dorian began. "How do you stay so positive? I get so depressed when I go for an interview and I don't get the job, but not you."

"Dorian, all I can say is that I grew up in a house where I was taught that I can do anything that I want, to step out on faith and take risks for things that are important to me. So I know if I work hard and keep the faith that anything is possible."

"It is true too," Ivory said, picking up her cape and throwing it around her shoulders.

"Aren't there times when a person does all that and they still don't get the breaks that they strive so hard for?" Dorian asked.

"Of course," Rayanne said.

"Then what?" Dorian asked.

"Dorian, when you put everything you have got into what you are doing and it doesn't work out, then it wasn't meant to be. It's as simple as that," Rayanne said.

"And you can accept it as that?" Dorian rubbed the side of her head.

"Sure I can, but I don't give up," Rayanne said and she stopped typing. "What blessings God has for me, nothing or no one can block them, but I do believe we have to pay our dues."

Dorian moved her head up and down. "You are so focused, so centered."

"Because I'm doing exactly what I want to do. I love writing. Writing is my passion. I never felt this way when I was acting. Writing is a whole different feeling and I'm going to succeed at it. It may not happen for a hundred years, but it will happen," Rayanne laughed. "I take that back. It had better be soon because I need to pay for this computer."

Rayanne had taken out a third credit card and bought the computer. It was taking too much out of her to write it all on paper and she would have to transcribe it later, so she made the sacrifice and got the computer. She would just continue to pay the minimum on each card until she could do better.

"Do you need us to bring you anything?" Dorian asked.

"No, thanks. You guys have fun," Rayanne said, her fingers racing over the keyboard, her creative juices flowing again.

"Well, we'll see you later," Dorian said.

"See you later," Ivory said, going toward the door and looking over her shoulder. "And we won't tell you what you missed."

Rayanne didn't stop typing until she had finished the script. "It's done," she said, eyes closed, her back against the chair. The script took longer than she thought, but she was glad it was finished.

Rayanne thought of Lionel. He'd called earlier and asked her to meet him at the Karaoke Bar when she finished her script. She looked at her watch, then reached for the phone and dialed his number. Although the hour was late and he still wanted to see her, Rayanne begged off, promising to see him tomorrow. He argued, but Rayanne prevailed and felt a sense of relief at the thought of going to bed one night before midnight.

One hour later, Rayanne emerged from the Madison Avenue Copy Shop, armed with five copies of her script, and before returning home, she stopped off and had a hot dog and a cup of herbal tea. In the morning she'd take a copy of the script to the Writers Guild, mail one copy each to three major production companies, and wait.

As it turned out, the call she waited for, hoped for, would've done anything for, didn't come, and of course, she was disappointed because although she'd written many plays, that was the one that she really felt good about. Writing the plays was easy. The characters she created were so fresh, so alive. They were like her best friends. The difficult part was shopping the plays. After many meetings and luncheons, rejections and disappointments, Rayanne decided that she would take the advice of her roommates as well as others. She'd get an agent.

Chapter 4

Getting an agent was just as difficult as finding a publisher. The same response was given. "We are currently not accepting any new clients. We hope you will be successful in placing your project with another company. Thank you for thinking of us." That was the usual story. At least that was the response that Rayanne got when she tried to shop her own scripts, but she never gave up. She'd always believed that nothing worth having came easily and that perseverance brought results.

It was Friday evening. Ivory and Dorian were going to the Apollo Theater for a show. Rayanne was working on another script.

"I'll catch you guys on Wednesday night for the amateur competition," Rayanne said, looking up from the computer, as Dorian and Ivory were leaving.

"Okay," Dorian replied. "See you later."

"Later," Ivory said and closed the door behind them.

Rayanne liked going to the Apollo Theater, especially on Wednesday for the amateur night. So much talent came through that theater. That was the place where many stars were born.

The computer was set up at the far end of the den. There were nights when Rayanne would sit there and become emerged in the characters she created, characters whose lives she breathed energy, compassion, and humor into. She felt a real connection with those characters, unlike the characters she portrayed as an actress. These characters were truly like members of her family.

Rayanne found through writing that she could visit places she'd never been and perhaps would never go to but would read about such places and tour them only in her mind. For hours she'd put her personal spin on the issues of the world and leave the problems of the real world, such as hunger, abuse, violence, and things like those, behind.

Rayanne got up from the computer, got a bottle of water from the refrigerator, and called her parents. When she started typing again, she revised several chapters and drafted one more. It was after midnight when she turned off the computer and took a relaxing bubble bath. Rayanne always took a pad and pen into the bathroom with her and while sitting in the bubbles, she made notes for another chapter on another script.

When the phone rang, she picked it up from the floor and answered it.

"Rayanne, are you still sitting at that computer?" Lionel asked.

"No, the bathtub," she replied.

"Want someone to wash your back? I come cheap."

"Lionel, I've been meaning to talk with you."

"What about?"

"I don't think we should see each other anymore."

"Why? What did I do?"

"Nothing," Rayanne said, closing her eyes and sighing deeply. "Lionel, you've been great, but I can't give you what you want. I'm so committed to my writing that I don't have time for hardly anything else."

"I don't want to lose you, Rayanne. I care about you."

"I care about you too."

"But only as a friend."

"Yes, Lionel," Rayanne said, and when they hung up, she felt sad. Without meaning to she'd hurt Lionel. She couldn't offer him the kind of relationship he wanted, and she felt guilty.

Rayanne got out of the tub and took her pad and pen into the bedroom. Once in bed, she stared up at the ceiling before finally drifting into a horrible nightmare. She'd dreamed that her father had died. The dream seemed so real, it left her shaken.

Rayanne turned over in bed, finding the sheets wrapped tightly around her body. She peeled them away and looked at the clock. It was 4:45 and had it not been so early, she would've called her parents again to make sure everything was all right. She got out of bed and was on her way to the kitchen for a cold drink when she saw Ivory letting Cal out. Not only had Ivory started seeing Cal again, but he'd been staying overnight. But what was even more amazing was the frequency in which Henry had stayed the night with Dorian. How did he ever manage to explain his absences to his wife?

At six o'clock that morning, knowing her parents were early risers, Rayanne picked up the phone and dialed their number. Shortly afterward, she was being assured that all was well with her family. She returned to bed and lay still, happy that it was Saturday, and she didn't have to go off to work. She was still very tired.

Rayanne got up again a few hours later. She was having a cup of coffee when Dorian joined her in the kitchen.

"You missed a great show last night," Dorian said, filling a cup with coffee, but Rayanne didn't respond. "Rayanne, did you hear me?"

"What does Henry tell Olympia when he spends the night with you?" Rayanne asked.

"Where is that coming from?" Dorian asked with a frown.

"Dorian, if Henry can cheat so easily on his wife with you, don't you think he'll do the same with you if the two of you eventually end up together?"

"Rayanne, we've been all through this. Henry and I love each other and we're going to be together, forever."

"Who's gonna be together forever?" Ivory asked, breezing into the room and getting a cup for coffee.

"Henry and I," Dorian replied.

"Are we talking about Mr. Senior Citizen again?" Ivory chuckled.

"I've got a bone to pick with you also, Ivory," Rayanne said.

Ivory turned with a surprised look on her face. "Me?" she asked.

"Yes, you. I saw Cal leaving this morning. I just don't feel comfortable having him around so much," Rayanne said.

"Is Lionel giving you any? You seem so edgy lately." Ivory laughed.

"I've not been sleeping well and no, Lionel is not giving me any. In fact he had never given me any, and I ended it with him last night," Rayanne said.

"Now I see why you're so bitchy," Ivory said.

"Oh, Rayanne, why? Lionel is a really nice guy," Dorian said.

"I know that but it just didn't work out," Rayanne said. "But back to the two of you, both of you are in no-win situations. I hope you know that and you really should do something about it."

"Well, I'm staying in mine and that's settled," Dorian said, sitting at the table with her coffee.

"I told you Rayanne can be an old mother hen," Ivory said, sipping coffee from her cup.

On Tuesday afternoon, Dorian opened the door and stormed into the loft wearing a pair of designer jeans and a white blouse with the sleeves rolled up. Her hair was loosely pinned up in a ponytail that trailed down her back. She threw her portfolio onto the couch and dropped down beside it.

"Hey, Dorian," Ivory said from the floor where she was sitting and counting her money.

"Hey, girl," Rayanne said, looking up from her computer.

Dorian seemed distracted. She kicked off her shoes and rubbed her feet.

"Dorian, is something wrong?" Rayanne asked, shutting off the computer and getting up to go over and talk with her.

"I didn't get the assignment," Dorian said, folding her arms across her chest. "I wanted that shoot so badly."

"I know," Rayanne said, sitting beside Dorian,

seeing her disappointment. "There'll be other jobs, better ones even."

"The same thing happened to me a couple of weeks ago. The owner of Jazzy Modeling Agency told me she would have hired me on the spot if I had several good head shots in my portfolio. I don't know what's wrong with me. Instead of giving my money to Cal, I could have had all the shots that I needed. But, my mistake, I'm not going to worry about that now," Ivory said. "How about this? Why don't we get some of that great Chinese food that you like so much and a bottle of wine and celebrate?"

Ivory took out two bills, placed them to the side, and put the other bills back into the small square box and rushed off with the box to her room.

"What are we celebrating?" Dorian called out after her.

"Life, us being together, everything. What difference does it make?" Ivory said, returning to the room. "So don't worry about it. Just hang in there."

Ivory called the Chinese restaurant and ordered food for them.

Dorian had been so accustomed to getting what she wanted, but the rejection had left her visibly affected, or was it something else that had Dorian troubled?

Ivory saw that Dorian still had a perplexed look on her face. "Something else bothering you?"

"If I don't get a handle on that math, I won't graduate." Dorian wrinkled up her face.

"Math?" Ivory asked. "Is that what's bothering you? Get your book."

"Are you good at math?" Dorian asked, a little

surprised. She knew Ivory was smart but had no idea that math was one of her better subjects.

"Ivory is a mathematical genius," Rayanne put in as Dorian rushed off to get her book. When she returned, she sat on the floor beside Ivory, and they began to work on some of the problems.

Rayanne resumed typing.

After a while, Dorian slapped the book shut. "I think I've got it," she said and after a moment, she said, "Olympia was waiting for me downstairs."

"You lying," Ivory said.

"Did she say something to you?" Rayanne asked, getting up from behind her computer and going over to join the girls.

"She told me she knew I was seeing her husband and if I didn't break it off with him, I'd be sorry," Dorian said.

"Dog," Ivory said.

"What did she mean by that?" Rayanne asked.

"Sounds like a threat to me," Ivory said. "What are you going to do?"

"Dorian, we've told you time and time again that you need to cut Henry out of your life. All he's going to bring you is trouble. See what just happened? It could be worse next time. Get rid of him," Rayanne said.

Dorian began to cry. "I don't know if I can."

"Of course you can. If you are afraid of being alone, you don't have to worry about that with all those guys out there who would die to date you," Rayanne said.

"Cut your losses, girl, and move on before we find you in a garbage can somewhere," Ivory said.

"Ivory," Rayanne scolded.

"We'll just have to be more careful," Dorian said

with such a defiant look that they didn't pursue the matter further that night.

Ivory thought it was best to change the subject. "I got a new job."

"Really? I didn't know you were looking for a new job," Rayanne said.

"Neither did I," Dorian said.

"Well, I needed to make more money, and this job pays better, so a lot more money will be coming in, so there," Ivory replied.

"Where?" Dorian asked.

"Over at Jacko's," Ivory said.

"I hear the tips are good there too," Dorian said.

"But better than that, I get to wear one of those cute little sexy outfits." Ivory grinned.

"When do you start?" Rayanne asked.

"Tomorrow," Ivory said.

"Tomorrow?" Rayanne looked at Ivory, a wrinkle in her brow. "Did you give notice at your old job?"

"No, but I think they'll notice that I'm gone when I don't show up anymore," Ivory laughed.

"Girl, you're too much," Rayanne laughed also.

"Let's go to LaVoice's tonight," Dorian said.

"LaVoice's?" Ivory's ears stood up with interest.

LaVoice's was one of the hottest, poshest clubs in the city that was frequented by Hollywood types and professional athletes, and Ivory had wanted to go there from the time she'd heard about it. She got up and put a stack of CDs back into the case and returned to the couch.

"What's going on there?" Ivory asked.

"They are having a birthday party," Dorian said, "and we are invited."

"You lying. Whose chain did you pull?" Ivory asked, looking at Dorian with a sly smile.

"I got the hookup, girl," Dorian joked, apparently recovered from her earlier shock.

"No lie," Ivory agreed.

"What kind of place is this LaVoice's?" Rayanne asked.

"It's a place where young, hip, energetic people as well as established businesspeople get together and hang out. I understand that all kinds of huge deals are initiated with contacts right there in that club. It is one of those exclusive, private clubs and it is really off the freaking hook," Dorian said. "It's up on the West Side, and it's a fabulous place."

"Whoa," Rayanne said. "So, are we going?"

"If you guys want to go," Dorian replied.

"Well, like Ivory said, whose chain did you pull to get us into a club like that?" Rayanne asked.

"We are the Manhattan Trio and we are pretty darn hot, so who is going to refuse us? So, you guys want to go?"

"Why not? It's something to do," Ivory answered, and of course she was joking because Ivory would have given her eyetooth to go to that club.

When a song played that each of the girls liked, they got up and began dancing all around the room. After dancing to several more tunes, they collapsed on the floor.

"Ivory, please get me some water," Rayanne joked, using the back of her hand to wipe perspiration from her forehead.

"Hell, you better go get me some," Ivory chuckled, but she rolled over on the floor and got up. "Dorian, you want some water?"

Ivory returned with two bottles of water. Dorian was on the floor, staring up at the ceiling.

"Henry and I had a talk last night," Dorian commented.

"Forgive me if I don't applaud, but don't you two talk, like, every second? What am I missing here?" Ivory asked, and she snickered. Only Dorian did not share the humor. "Well?" Ivory took another sip from her water bottle.

"Ivory, shut up," Rayanne said, concerned that Dorian's mood had suddenly changed again.

"What did I say?" Ivory asked.

"Just shut up, will you?" Rayanne said to one girl, then to the other. "Go on, Dorian. What did you and Henry talk about?"

"I know we have been through this before, but he said once again that he's asking Olympia for a divorce," Dorian announced.

"Do you think that was the reason for Olympia's visit today?" Rayanne asked.

"No shit. Do you think he's really getting a divorce?" Ivory asked.

"That's what he said," Dorian said.

Dorian had met Henry one morning when she was having breakfast at a coffee shop in Manhattan. Henry approached her table, asked if he could join her, and she said yes. Henry was so taken by Dorian's beauty that after they'd had lunch at an elegant Midtown restaurant, they walked in Central Park, and they talked. Time led them into dinner and before they parted that evening, she'd learned that Henry was a business tycoon. In addition to his owning a magazine company, there was also a house on Long Island, a summer place on Martha's Vineyard, as well as other real estate.

Henry learned that Dorian had arrived in New York alone several months earlier. She told him perhaps she'd attend a community college and take some courses. She wasn't sure what she wanted to do with her life, no direction. She had no friends or family in the city. She'd not shared much more than that. She'd not told him where she'd come from, where her family was, or whether there was any contact between them.

Henry was satisfied with what little information she gave him. He fell in love with her and he wanted her and that was enough for him. When they met, he did tell her he was married, but that the marriage was on the rocks. Since Dorian wasn't looking for a husband of her own at the time, him being married was fine with her. But since that time, her priorities had changed.

"This is what you want, isn't it?" Rayanne asked.

"Yes. I love Henry," Dorian replied. "I want to be with him."

"Well, it's about damn time," Ivory said.

"Yes," Dorian considered, "I think so." She knew she loved Henry, but there were times when she questioned whether she was in love with him.

"You think so?" Ivory questioned, looking intently at Dorian. "If this man gets a divorce from his wife, he's gonna want a commitment from you, so you had better be sure this is what you want."

"I know that," Dorian answered slowly.

"You do love him, don't you?" Rayanne asked.

"Yes," Dorian replied.

"You know you don't love that old-ass man," Ivory said.

"What difference does it make how old the man is? As long as he loves and respects you, he treats you well, and makes you happy. All that good stuff," Rayanne said.

"If I thought Dorian and Henry were really serious about this relationship, I would have a different attitude," Ivory said. "I think Dorian is all about the money Henry gives her. There it is. That's what I think and Henry, well, he acts like he loves Dorian, but for years I didn't see him doing a damn thing to bring him and Dorian together as a couple. Sure, he sneaks around and sees her every chance he gets, but he is no closer to getting a divorce than he was last year."

"Ivory, don't you dare go there," Dorian said.

Rayanne had always wondered why a girl as young and beautiful and who had so much going for her would depend so much on Henry. He was a nice man, a generous man, but he wasn't an attractive one and he was much older than Dorian. Although it appeared that Henry was very wealthy, Dorian had the potential to do well on her own. Rayanne would be the first to admit that there was nothing wrong with a girl looking out for her future, but Dorian's dependency on Henry appeared to be so much more.

"Dorian, you're high maintenance and he gives you what you want, but Henry is perfectly satisfied with the situation just the way it is," Ivory said.

"Your behind," Dorian said.

"But you know I'm right," Ivory said.

Dorian shrugged her shoulders just as the doorbell rang. Ivory answered it. Minutes later, they were seated at the table, enjoying their dinner.

"Rayanne, what would make you happy?" Dorian asked.

Rayanne sat silently for a moment. Then she answered, "When I get a buyer for one of my plays. That will make me happy."

"You heard the way she phrased that, didn't you?" Ivory asked, wiping her mouth and getting up to get more napkins. "She said when she gets a buyer for one of her plays, not if but when. That's what she said, and I swear to God, when she gets a buyer for one play, they are gonna pull everything she's ever written. Just wait and see. It's gonna be the start of something big."

"That sounds good to me," Rayanne said and smiled, hoping everything would turn out just the way Ivory had described it.

"I believe it," Ivory said. "It's true. There are people out there who've been writing for years and then, one will hit. Then they sell everything they've written. I heard that sometimes these industry power suits will buy a story before the book is written, a proposal." Ivory smiled. "Look at us, Dorian will soon graduate and when I get the break I'm looking for, we're gonna be cooking with gas."

"Hello," Dorian said and reached over to give Ivory five.

"So, what are you whores wearing tonight?" Ivory asked.

"Whores? I beg your pardon," Rayanne said.

"Well, we probably will be before we decide to settle down with one man," Ivory said.

"Speak for yourself," Dorian said.

"Hell no, I'm speaking for all of us," Ivory said.

"That we all will be whores before we get married, Ivory, please," Rayanne said. "You can't be serious." She looked at Ivory, whose face was as serious as she'd ever seen it. Then she asked with raised eyebrows, "Ivory, do you really believe that?" and laughed a little.

"No, gal," Ivory said.

"Then why do you say things like that?" Rayanne sighed.

"Because it makes me feel good," Ivory giggled.

"Speaking of marriage," Dorian said, "we're going to be in each other's weddings, right?"

"Of course we are, but why are we talking about that now?" Rayanne wanted to know why Dorian was suddenly so preoccupied with all of them getting married. There was plenty of time for that.

"Unless someone here is pregnant. Is someone pregnant in here?" Ivory asked, looking from Dorian to Rayanne.

"My vibrator would make medical history if all of a sudden it became somebody's baby's daddy," Rayanne chuckled.

"You still wearing that thing out, girl?" Ivory laughed, giving Rayanne the high five.

"Every chance I get," Rayanne chuckled.

"Do you oil that bad boy down?" Ivory asked.

"Damn, you hoochies are sick," Dorian laughed.

"Might be, but I am not horny." Rayanne grinned. "Now, answer the question, are you pregnant, Dorian?"

"No, I'm not, but I think we should at least think about it. We don't have to wait until we're old to start planning," Dorian said.

"Dorian, what gives? A little while ago I was under the impression that you weren't in a hurry to get married. What happened in the last half hour that changed your mind?" Ivory asked.

"Well, the thought sort of goes and comes," Dorian said.

Rayanne said, "I would like to catch a good man before I'm too old and ugly to attract one, but I'm not in a hurry."

"You don't have to worry about that. You know that black girls have the kind of skin that looks really great for a long time," Dorian said.

"What the hell is she talking about now?" Ivory said to Rayanne. Then to Dorian, "Dorian, you're so damn gorgeous that you'll probably look good after you've been dead and buried a hundred years."

"Ain't that the truth?" Rayanne agreed.

Dorian said, "We aren't getting any younger."

Ivory got up and cleared the table and Rayanne walked over to the fish tank and dropped several pieces of fish food into the water. She went back to the couch and picked up an apple from the bowl that sat on the coffee table. She wiped it off on her shirt and took a bite out of it.

Ivory and Dorian looked at Rayanne with raised eyebrows. She had just polished off a good serving of Chinese food, now an apple. Rayanne, reading each girl's thought, said, "Huh-uh, I'm not pregnant. I just want this apple. I think it's emotional eating."

"I just don't want to be the one left alone," Dorian said, her beautiful eyes sad.

"What are you talking about?" Rayanne asked, eyeing Dorian.

"We're family, right?" Dorian asked, and Rayanne and Ivory looked briefly at each other.

"Yes, we are and that's not going to change," Rayanne assured her. "We love you, silly."

"Do you want us to carve that in stone?" Ivory smiled.

Dorian didn't answer; she just smiled at both girls, and that smile touched her eyes and a twinkle replaced the sadness that was there previously.

Ivory looked from one girl to the other with a straight face and said, "Well, my question is back on the table. What are you bitches wearing this evening?"

"Oh, Jesus," Rayanne said.

"She's incorrigible. What can I say?" Dorian said, and they fell out laughing.

Chapter 5

They arrived at the party, each wearing a tight, knit minidress. Each girl had dashed to and from one another's vanity, selecting matching accessories, nail polish, nylons, whatever was necessary to complete her outfit that evening. Rayanne took Dorian's berry-berry red nail polish and did her nails to match the lipstick that she'd be wearing. Those colors would be a perfect match for the bloodred dress she had selected. Dorian borrowed a pair of midnight-blue nylons to wear with her navy blue dress, and Ivory rummaged through Rayanne's and Dorian's trays until she'd found just the right pair of earrings and hair clip to accessorize her white outfit.

They'd gone to numerous parties, discos, and other functions and had danced their nights away, getting by with not more than a couple of hours of sleep a night, but they'd loved it. Each girl was different, each had her own agenda, but they meshed and got along like a well-oiled machine. They'd formed a bond; they were like family. Wherever they went, they caused a stir. They were poised and elegant and they were beautiful.

The next hours at the party were interesting, and although they ran into several acquaintances, they met a multitude of new people, some athletes, some actors, but mostly enterprising businesspeople.

Rayanne had danced until she was dizzy before returning to the table. She sat and sipped thirstily on her drink, and watched as Ivory and Dorian continued to dance. *Those girls have stamina*, Rayanne thought, and laughed. Then she noticed a man who'd been pestering Ivory most of the evening. He was tapping her on the shoulder again, asking for a dance. Ivory was dancing and smiling until she saw who it was. Then her smile faded. She continued to dance with the partner with whom she'd gone out onto the dance floor, ignoring the pest. Rayanne turned her attention elsewhere. Everyone was having a good time and she thought how perfect her life was. She couldn't ever remember being happier. She was sharing a wonderful home with two very dear friends, she had a decent job and was living in one of the most glamorous, exciting cities in all the world. This was a perfect picture; she was young, life was free and great, and she would have it forever.

Rayanne was first joined at the table by Ivory, who was perspiring and touching her forehead lightly with her hand. She grabbed her purse and rushed off to the ladies' room. Dorian, however, returned to the table looking as fresh as a daisy, took one sip from her frosty drink, and immediately returned to the dance floor, where she disappeared into the crowd. Ivory returned to the table shortly after having freshened up. "This is a nice party," she said.

"I'll say," Rayanne agreed, thinking it was the nicest party she'd ever attended, and there was something to be said about the caliber of people in attendance. This was a group of affluent people, and from snatches of conversations, Rayanne knew that these were powerful people in big businesses and she definitely wanted to be a part of that.

"That must be the birthday girl," Ivory said as a young pretty blonde entered with an escort and was greeted at the door by several people yelling happy birthday.

Rayanne looked around and asked, "Where?" as the lights of several cameras went off and took pictures of the couple.

"Where are your glasses, Grandma?" Ivory asked.

"I don't wear glasses," Rayanne said.

"Well, you must need them because they're right over there," Ivory said, nodding her head in the direction of the couple and the flashing lights.

She's either the birthday girl or some celebrity, Rayanne thought, and she said after observing the couple, "I think they make a good-looking couple, don't you?"

"No, I think they're all wrong for each other," Ivory said, thinking the guy could do a lot better. Rayanne was at a loss. She didn't see anything wrong with the girl. She looked at Ivory, who lifted her shoulders and said, "She looks fake and cheap, that's what's wrong, but as they say, there's no accounting for taste."

"Ivory, don't be such a wuss," Rayanne said.

"I just said the chick looks cheap and fake."

"And I disagree."

"I'm glad we agreed long ago that it was okay to disagree." Ivory giggled.

Dorian returned to the table. They chatted, observed couples dancing, as well as the arrival of some latecomers.

Ivory's pest returned and tapped her on her shoulder. When she turned to see who it was, she dropped her head to the table. Rayanne and Dorian ignored their intruder.

When Ivory lifted her head, the man was still there. She paused to draw in a deep breath, and she closed her eyes, hard-pressed to know whether she should scream in frustration or be happy at the thought that this might just be the man who would be at the receiving end of one of her cruel pranks at the end of the evening.

Although she began to figure the pest into her plans for later, Ivory realized she still had to keep up her little charade, pretending not to want to be bothered with him, yet not letting him get away completely. Ivory opened her eyes and through clenched teeth with eyes rolled toward the ceiling, she said, "I can't believe this is happening to me. How can this be happening to me? Why is this happening to me?" The man wasn't a bad-looking guy. As a matter of fact, he was very attractive, but he acted like he wrote the book on stupidity. Ivory loved men, all men, but she didn't have much use for stupid ones. "What do you want now?" A sound of irritation caught in her throat.

"The American flag, I see," he said. "Red, white, and blue." The girls looked up at him. "The way you're dressed, I mean," he said. The girls looked at each other, lifting their shoulders in a helpless gesture. "I'd like to dance with you," he said to Ivory.

"Why?" she asked, suppressing a groan of aggravation.

"Why not?" he countered.

"I don't want to dance, so would you please leave me alone?" Ivory said, drew in a slow breath, and brushed a piece of hair from her cheek with a brief movement.

"Just one dance, and I promise I won't bother you anymore," he said.

That guy doesn't take no for an answer, Rayanne thought. *He'd better hope that Ivory doesn't go off on him.*

"You're drop-dead gorgeous, you know. You are one fine mama," he continued, and he was right because Ivory looked exceptionally so that evening, but this man was exasperating.

Ivory said, "Get over it, will you?"

"I'm serious. You're beautiful," he insisted.

"Thank you very much. Now, will you please just leave me alone?" Ivory said. "My friends and I are trying to enjoy ourselves, okay?"

The young man stared admiringly at Ivory. He looked from Rayanne to Dorian and asked, "What about you ladies? Care to dance?"

"No, thanks," Rayanne said, looking away. He looked at Dorian with the question in his eyes.

"No, but thanks," Dorian said politely.

The man looked at Ivory again. She clicked her teeth and turned away from him. Then he said to her, "Baby, if you could see yourself as others do, you'd kiss yourself." He paused a moment. "Why won't you dance with me? You've danced with every Tom, Dick, and Harry in the place. What's wrong with me?" he asked, refusing to be offended by the rejection he received.

"For one thing, you ain't Tom, Dick, or Harry. Besides, I'm tired and I just don't want to dance anymore," Ivory said, faking a smile.

"Am I supposed to feel sorry for you?" he asked.

Ivory looked up at the ceiling again. She moistened her lips and gazed into the young man's eyes. She said, "Feel sorry for me? Of course I don't want you to feel sorry for me."

"Guilty, then?" he asked, and without wavering, he returned her gaze.

She gave a short laugh and shook her head. "No, guilt requires a conscience and I'll just bet you don't have one of those."

With that he dropped his head, laughed, and said, "I'm glad you have a sense of humor."

"What would you know about it?" Ivory murmured under her breath and thought, *He's gonna be a wonderful victim*, but it was becoming increasingly more difficult getting to the end of the evening. The man was absolutely tiresome. "Who let you in anyway?" she asked.

"Okay, okay. I get the picture," he said, and with that, the young man turned and walked slowly away, which took Ivory by surprise. Then the man turned a moment to say, "Damn, you're fine, though." With that, he walked away.

"It's about time," Dorian said.

Ivory clicked her teeth. Rayanne looked at her and was a little confused by Ivory's expression. Rayanne knew she'd been trying to get rid of the guy all evening, but now that he was gone, she seemed disturbed. There was a reason for that, Rayanne was certain. She just didn't know what it was.

At midnight, a waiter appeared with a platter that held a cake with nineteen candles lit. He stopped at the table where the young blonde, her escort, and two other couples were sitting. The club was suddenly filled with voices singing "Happy Birthday." Afterward, they ate cake and drank champagne.

Rayanne met and shared her aspirations with a number of people. Some took her phone number with a promise to assist her with her career and some just promised to call. She excused herself and went to the powder room. On her way, she noticed a tall, well-built, handsome man with an air of confidence, having a drink at the bar.

"Ummm," Rayanne said under her breath. When she was making her way back to her table, a wonderful, totally surprising thing happened. The man approached her.

"Hello," he said after taking a moment to look her over carefully. He had a deep, sexy voice, nice broad shoulders, and damn, he smelled good too. He had a medium brown complexion and a smile that he wore only too well. He was the epitome of Corporate America. He guided the cigarette that he was holding to his lips, and took a draw. He turned his head away and blew out a puff of smoke. "How are you this evening, Miss Wilson?" His smile revealed white teeth. He took her left hand, looked at her fingers, and said, "I take it you're not married, or did you remove your ring for the evening?"

This man definitely has sex appeal, she thought, withdrawing her hand.

"I don't believe we've been introduced," she said, looking up into his eyes, slightly taken aback, aware of a powerful jolt of attraction that rushed through her at his touch.

"You're Rayanne Wilson, aren't you?" he asked. "And a lovely creature you are."

"Yes, but I'm sorry to say that you have me at a disadvantage. I don't have any idea who you are."

Ralph Underwood introduced himself and said he knew she'd done some acting, was an aspiring writer, and he bet she was damn good at it too.

"Ho, ho, ho," she said. "A frustrated writer, you forgot to add."

"I'm sure that will change."

"You think so, huh?"

"Oh yeah."

"Let's hope so."

"Nothing is impossible," he said, taking her hand in his again. "So, tell me, Miss Wilson, are you married?"

"Are you sure you don't already know? You seem to know everything else about me."

"Actually, I really don't know that much, but I'd like to. As a matter of fact, I'd like nothing better. You certainly are a lovely creature." He paused. "Am I repeating myself?"

"No, I'm not married, thank you very much, and yes, you are repeating yourself," she said, and was surprised at just how much she was enjoying the attention of this man.

"Are you here alone?"

"No, I'm here with friends," Rayanne said, but she was sure he already knew that.

"Boyfriend?" he questioned.

"No, girlfriends." She went along with him.

"Good, then perhaps there's a chance that you and I can become better acquainted."

"That might be nice," she said. Rayanne knew that Ralph was older than she and the men she'd dated in the past, but he was extremely handsome, intelligent, and he had a wonderful smile. She looked around the room, and when she looked at him again, he was staring at her. "Is something wrong?" she asked, a crease in her brow.

"Nothing from where I am standing."

"Then why are you looking at me that way?"

"What way is that?" he asked. She looked at him unsmiling, and although she didn't answer him, if she were to guess, she'd say he had something devious on his mind. She glanced away from the look in his dark eyes. "Okay, okay," he said, lifting a hand into the air. "You got me. I'll admit it. I was saying to myself, 'self, I bet under all that calm beats the heart of a wild, wanton woman.' Does that come close to what you thought I was thinking?" he asked, an amused expression on his handsome face.

Dirty old man, she thought, and was about to walk away. "Good night, Mr. Underwood."

"You're not leaving?" he said.

"I'm going back to join my friends."

"May I join you and your friends?"

"If you'd like, if you think you can behave yourself."

"I'll be the perfect gentleman."

As the evening wore on, Rayanne found herself talking easily to Ralph Underwood about her work, her goals, and her family. In the meantime, she'd learned that he was thirty-five, a native New Yorker, and a successful stockbroker at a Wall Street firm. He appeared to be fun-loving, energetic, and charming. He had a real passion for life.

It turned out that Ralph and Dorian knew each other. They'd met at a party some time ago and had run into each other on occasions, but they didn't know each other well.

Into the evening Ralph said, "Ladies, there was this guy over at the bar who told me you all treated him really cold."

"Which guy was that?" Rayanne asked.

"Some guy over at the bar. He just walked up to me and started talking," Ralph said, a twinkle in his eyes.

"Maybe he had it coming to him," Ivory said.

"He must've because I find you ladies charming," Ralph commented.

"That's what some of them say," Ivory said.

"And others, what do they say?" Ralph asked.

"Something much worse," Ivory said, and Ralph looked questioningly and Ivory replied, "Probably that we're ladies with attitudes."

"Now, that's thought-provoking," Ralph said, and returned his attention to Rayanne.

Before he could ask, she said, lifting a hand, "You don't want to know what I think. We love people, we love to have a good time, but we choose who we want to have a good time with. He wasn't one of our choices."

Ralph nodded.

"Really, though, we're not that bad," Rayanne assured him.

"I didn't think you were," Ralph said, pushed his chair back, and asked Rayanne to dance. She accepted, and when they came together on the dance floor, they moved as though they'd danced together for years. He held her gently at first, but as they swayed to the music, his arms tightened around her waist and he became lost in the music.

"Are you married?" Rayanne asked.

"What?" he said, caught up in the music and the feel of Rayanne's body against his.

"Do you have a wife?" she said, pushing back enough so she could look into his eyes.

"No, not exactly," he responded, pulling her close so that her face rested against his. When he didn't clarify his response, she pulled her head back to look at him again. "I was involved," he began, and stopped.

"Was?" she questioned.

"Was," he said without further explanation.

"What is your present situation in the romance department?"

"I don't have a present situation."

"What about the woman you were involved with? Where's she now? The relationship just didn't work?"

"Something like that," he said. *Here we go again*, Rayanne thought, annoyed. She wasn't sure why Ralph was so open about some phases of his life but so tight-lipped about others. Ralph, seeing the look on her face, said, "Are you upset with me?"

She wasn't upset, but she was puzzled as to why Ralph wouldn't tell her anything about his personal life.

"I've been talking about myself from the time I joined you and your friends this evening."

"I know, all business. I'd like to know something about you, who you are, what's important to you, your likes, dislikes. Things like that."

"There really isn't much to tell," he said, but she was certain that a man like Ralph could write a book. "My life hasn't been as fascinating as you might think."

"I'd like to be the judge of that." She smiled warmly, looked into his eyes, and that look made Ralph want to grant her every wish.

"Well, I was married. It didn't work out. I lived with a woman for a while and we had a child. It didn't work either, but all that was a very long time ago."

"What happened?"

"It's a long story," he said.

More secrets, she thought, and Ralph looked at Rayanne for what seemed a long time, but actually, it was only seconds. He said, "I was married once for a short while. After the marriage failed, I lived with a woman and we had a child. I dated another woman whom I just recently broke up with. She wanted more than I could give, so we thought it best to go our separate ways. She was a nice lady. It just didn't work out. Right now I'm on my own. End of story."

"What happened to the child?" she asked and watched as a sad look came into his eyes.

"My daughter and her mother were killed in an automobile accident, and," he said sadly, "if you don't mind, I'd rather not talk about this tonight."

Rayanne was immediately sorry she'd pressed and she told him so.

"How could you've known? It doesn't show, right?" Ralph said, suddenly joking and just as sudden, he became serious again. "I suppose you could say that I've been unlucky in love."

"It seems you've had your share of tragedies. Are you okay?" Rayanne said, noticing how the sadness had now covered his eyes. It seemed she'd opened old wounds without meaning to.

"Yeah," he said, then asked, "What about you? You've put me through the third degree, so now I'd like to hear more about you. Is there someone special in your life?"

"I just ended a situation as well. He wanted more than I could give, so we went our separate ways. It wasn't anything serious, though," she said.

That's soon to change, he thought and held her closer as they continued to dance. Rayanne closed her eyes, enjoying the music and the faint scent of the expensive aftershave Ralph was wearing. When she opened her eyes, she couldn't believe that the pest had returned to the table, and Ivory looked absolutely mortified. Rayanne smiled to herself, closed her eyes again, and continued to dance.

When that record was over and another played, she opened her eyes and was surprised to see Ivory being led onto the dance floor by the man whom she'd despised. It was another one of those slow songs and what surprised her more was what happened next. Ivory was dancing with her arms wrapped around the man's neck and running her fingers through that awful rat tail that hung from the back of his head. When the record was over and the girls returned to the table, Ivory didn't sit. She grabbed her purse and said, "We are leaving."

"We are?" Dorian asked, with raised eyebrows.

"What's wrong?" Ralph asked, and he looked from Ivory to Rayanne and back to Ivory.

"You know the guy that I was just dancing with?" Ivory said.

"The one you didn't like? What about him?" Ralph asked, but Rayanne was already out of her seat with her purse in her hand, as was Dorian. Ralph didn't understand why the sudden hurry to leave the club.

"I just Neeted him, so I'm getting the hell out of here," Ivory said, and the girls looked from one to the other and laughed.

Ralph was more puzzled than ever. "What's going on?" he asked.

"Ivory just put Neet on that guy's rat tail," Rayanne explained.

"Neet on his rat tail?" Ralph asked, disbelieving.

"That's right and if you all are coming with me, you'd better get a move on," Ivory said on her way toward the door.

Neet on the man's rat tail, Ralph thought, shaking his head as they left the club. *These ladies are something else.*

Rayanne allowed Ralph to see them home and he drove expertly through the busy streets. Ivory and Dorian said good night and entered the loft, while Rayanne and Ralph stood outside the door.

"You never did tell me how you knew so much about me," Rayanne said.

Ralph smiled. "I ran into Dorian after I saw you all together and I guess you could say I put her through the third degree."

"I see."

"You're so beautiful," Ralph said, looking down into Rayanne's face.

"I'm beginning to believe that you think so. You've been telling me that all evening."

"Then believe me. I've been devouring you with my eyes from the time I saw you, but do you know what I'd like to do more than anything else right now?"

Rayanne didn't answer. She stood against the door, looking up at him.

"I'd like to take you in my arms and kiss you. I've been wanting to all evening."

Rayanne still didn't speak.

"What do you think about that?"

"I don't think you'd be breaking any laws."

Ralph took the cue and gently pulled her away from the door. He took her face in his hands and let his lips brush hers ever so gently. He released her, looked into her eyes, and when he kissed her again, the kiss was more passionate. He sucked her lower lip into his mouth and ran his tongue over it, and when Rayanne's tongue darted into his mouth, his body jerked with an involuntary spasm.

When Ralph released Rayanne that time, she was dizzy, her head was spinning, and she could tell that he was affected by the kiss as well.

"I'd better go in now," she managed to say, her heart racing out of control.

"So soon?" he asked, kissing her again.

Suddenly, she began to wonder whether she was getting too carried away with this man. Who was he? What kind of man was he? What did she really know about him? She could be opening herself up for a major heartbreak. The heck, this man could be a serial killer.

"Yes, I really should," she said, as the hour was late and she did intend to go to church in the morning.

"Then, may I call you tomorrow?"

"I'd be disappointed if you didn't," she replied, trying to keep her voice steady.

Ralph really had an effect on her. He tried to kiss Rayanne again. She placed both hands up against his chest, but ignoring her protest, he pulled her to him and when his lips took possession of hers again, the kiss was fierce, demanding, and Rayanne closed her eyes and sighed with undisguised pleasure. The kiss went on until she was finally able to pull away.

"You will call me tomorrow," she said.

"Count on it." He lingered a moment longer, looking at her; then he was gone.

Rayanne entered the loft, stood for a moment with her back against the door, then joined the others in the living room.

"Come on over here, lover girl," Dorian teased, "and tell us all about it."

"Tell you what, dear?" Rayanne said, breezing into the room and plopping down on the couch.

"Yes," Ivory mimicked Rayanne, with a dreamy look in her eyes, "you will call me tomorrow." She then mimicked Ralph. "Count on it."

"Ivory," Rayanne said, sending a pillow in her direction, aware then that Ivory had been listening at the door.

"So, tell us about him," Ivory said.

"He's very nice. I like him," Rayanne said. Then she requested that Dorian tell her everything she knew about Ralph. Dorian shared that as far as she knew, he was a nice man, he wasn't married, she'd seen him around, sometimes with a woman, but never the same one twice, which made Rayanne think that maybe Ralph wasn't serious about anyone in particular. When Dorian told Rayanne what she knew about Ralph, Rayanne didn't know much more than what she'd learned from him.

"Come on. Stop trying to be so cool about this. I know your drawers are wet. Is he a good kisser?" Ivory asked.

"I hope so, because that's one thing that can turn me off in a hurry," Dorian said, crossing her legs and folding her arms across her chest.

"There isn't anything about Ralph that turns me off," Rayanne said, beaming.

"I take it he pleases you." Ivory gave her a sly smile.

Rayanne contained her enthusiasm as long as she could.

"Yes, Lord," she exclaimed, her hands up to her chest. "He's wonderful, simply wonderful." She was behaving like a schoolgirl and she knew it, but she didn't care. This was a first impression and there was something to be said about first impressions. If there was any truth in what they said about first impressions and if Ralph lived up to that impression, he'd be the kind of man she could do some serious bonding with.

Rayanne was glowing, Dorian and Ivory noticed. "I had a great time tonight, and I have never met anyone like Ralph." Rayanne smiled, thinking that it was sinful for her to be feeling that good about someone she'd just met. *Lord, just don't let him be a serial killer*, she thought.

"You ready to get with him?" Ivory asked.

"I bet you are. I would be, if I were you," Dorian said.

"But you ain't me and you ain't gonna get none a' that," Rayanne said, and more laughter ensued.

"Guess what, guys," Ivory said, going through her purse for a cigarette. She held a business card between her fingers as she lit the cigarette. She blew out a cloud of smoke. "I met a couple back at the club tonight. They have their own business, they are agents and they represent models. They said they handle some of the top models in New York." Dorian and Rayanne were excited. "She asked whether I'd ever done any modeling. I told her I'd done a little and they asked me to come in to see them. They said they were certain they could get some work for me. I told them I'm still working on that damn portfolio, but that I've got a good treatment." The words were rushing out of Ivory's mouth and when she paused a moment to think, she wished she'd had that portfolio completed.

"Yes, and I know you're gonna give it a shot," Dorian said gleefully.

"She said if I was interested, that I was to call for an appointment. She didn't seem to think the incomplete portfolio was a problem. Anyway, we'll see where it goes."

"It's important to have a good portfolio, but if they can work around it, that'll be great. Go for it, girl," Rayanne said.

"I agree," Dorian said, and she began to laugh.

"What's so funny?" Ivory asked. Dorian laughed some more. "What is it?"

"I was just thinking about the guy with the rat tail," Dorian said.

"I'm sure he's lost that miserable tail by now," Ivory said, and they talked more about the party, about how annoying their friend with the rat tail was and about Ralph. "Well, guys." Ivory stretched and yawned. "I think I'm gonna turn in."

"Me too," Rayanne said, and just as they were getting up to go to bed, the telephone rang. "Now, who can that be?" she said, hoping everything at home was fine.

The phone rang again. Ivory answered and handed it to Rayanne.

"Who is it?" Rayanne asked.

Ivory didn't respond. She just smiled. "See you in the morning, kiddo. Good night," she said.

Ivory looked at Dorian and whispered, "It's Ralph."

"Oooh," Dorian whispered back. "That didn't take long."

"Nope," Ivory agreed as the two of them went off to bed.

"Hello?" Rayanne said.

"I hope I didn't disturb anyone, but I had to speak to you before going to sleep," Ralph said.

"Hey," Rayanne said, and was pleased that she'd made as good an impression on Ralph as he had on her. It wasn't that she thought Ralph was out of her league, but he was so much more worldly and sophisticated than any of the other guys she had dated.

"You sound surprised."

"Ivory didn't say who was calling."

"Were you expecting someone else? I hope I didn't disappoint you."

Not only had he not disappointed her, but she was pleasantly surprised that he'd called so soon. When he said he'd call her tomorrow, she assumed the call would come later in the day, not at three in the morning, Rayanne thought, but she said with a smile, "No, not at all. Where are you?"

"At my apartment and I wish like hell you were here with me."

"Really?" Rayanne blushed.

"Yes, I do. I miss you already." He paused. "Tell me something. Do you miss me?"

"What kind of question is that?" she asked, and when she evaluated the question, the answer took her by surprise. She did miss him.

"It's simple and straightforward," he answered. "Do you?"

She inhaled softly. "You're putting me on the spot."

"Not really."

"I suppose I do miss you a little."

"That's good. Now, do you love me?" he pressed.

"I don't think so. What is this? Twenty questions."

"Do you always answer a question with a question?" he teased. Rayanne was silent. "It's not impossible, you know."

"No."

"No, you don't love me or no it's not impossible?"

"No, Ralph, it's not impossible for me to be in love with you, but—" she began, but Ralph interrupted.

"Don't answer it if you're going to say you don't love me, because honestly, I think I'm falling in love with you."

"We don't even know each other."

"I know what I like, and I like you. Right now that's enough for me."

"I like you too," Rayanne admitted.

"That's fine for now, but can we get together tomorrow and get to know each other better?"

"I think that can be arranged."

Rayanne went to bed and lay awake for what seemed like hours, her head filled with thoughts, thoughts of her future, how she'd go about making it happen, and pleasant thoughts of Ralph. When she finally did fall asleep, she slept like the dead.

Chapter 6

Rayanne was awakened on Sunday morning by a ringing telephone. It rang two more times before she reached for it and still she was too dazed to speak clearly. "Hello," she said.

"Rayanne?"

"Yes."

"Is this soon enough?" Ralph asked, sounding sexy.

"Yes, I suppose."

"Why don't you get yourself together and ride over to Jersey with me?"

"What's in Jersey?"

"I really just wanted to take you out for the day. We could enjoy the scenery, have breakfast somewhere in between, and just spend the day together. Hey, wait a minute," Ralph said, "let's back up a second. Good morning, beautiful."

"Good morning. How are you?" she asked, but she knew he was fine. At least his physical appearance was fine. The way he looked in that dark suit and the white pullover that clung to his muscular body when he removed his jacket after they'd danced was fresh in her mind.

"Fine. What kind of plans do you have for today?"

"Nothing much."

"That's good because I've got to see you, woman. I can't get you out of my mind."

"You can't?"

"Sure can't. So when can we get together?"

"Any time after two would be great."

"I thought you said you had no plans," he said, thinking six hours was too long to have to wait to see her.

"We're going to church but you're invited."

"To church?"

"Yes. You do go to church, don't you?"

"Yes, but I can't make it today."

"Okay, then, I'll see you this afternoon."

"Damn, I have to wait six whole hours to see you?" When Ralph was unsuccessful getting Rayanne to change her mind, he asked, "You go to church every Sunday?"

"I try to."

"And I can't change your mind?" he begged.

"I'm afraid not."

He paused a moment. "So, tell me, Miss Rayanne Wilson, did you enjoy the party last night?"

"It was great. I met some interesting people."

Ralph hoped he was one of the interesting ones.

"I find you interesting," he said.

"I'm just a country girl who was born and raised in the heart of South Carolina."

"I've heard that country girls make wonderful wives, mothers, and lovers."

"Don't forget that we have a host of other wonderful qualities."

"You're wonderful," he said softly into the phone. "I woke up this morning feeling very happy."

"Why was today an exception?"

"I met you last night, and the thought of you makes me happy."

"You know what that means, don't you? You need me in your life. My mother always told me that a person's needs dictate what makes him happy," she teased.

"You have a very wise mother."

"You get no argument from me."

"Rayanne, I've got a really serious question for you."

"What is it?"

"Have your feelings for me begun to resemble love?"

"We're not back to that again."

"You're just postponing the inevitable. You know that, don't you? Because I'm going to make you love me."

"You are something," she said, and looked at the clock on her night table. "It's getting late. I've got to get dressed so that I'm not late for church. I'll see you this afternoon, then?"

"Count on it," he said.

Rayanne went to church, but she didn't stay and talk with members afterward as she usually did. She took a taxi to the loft, changed into a pair of shorts and a top, and began preparing a simple meal. She was dashing around in the kitchen when Dorian and Ivory arrived. They changed and helped with the finishing touches, and when the food was ready the stove was left on just enough to keep dinner warm.

Rayanne took a quick shower and slipped into a shirt and top, applied a little makeup, and then waited for Ralph. When he hadn't arrived by four o'clock, Rayanne couldn't hide her disappointment. She never could hide her passion, and she was as passionate about her dislikes as her likes, and although she, Dorian, and Ivory thoroughly enjoyed the meal, including a bottle of champagne that Ivory bought to honor having put together enough money to complete her portfolio, Ralph was missed.

After eating, they walked around the block and at six thirty, Dorian and Ivory got dressed to go to an art showing that was being put on by a friend.

"Are you going to wait around here for Ralph?" Dorian asked.

"I want to get some work done, so I'll use this time to do it," Rayanne said.

"Liar," Ivory said. "You're gonna wait for Ralph. I wouldn't sit around and obsess over his ass. Hell, if that nigga stood me up, I wouldn't give him the time of day. He could've called, you know."

"That's right," Dorian agreed. "Frankly, I'm surprised he didn't."

Rayanne shrugged. "It's no big deal. Why are we talking about Ralph anyway?"

Ivory leaned over and put a comforting arm around Rayanne's shoulders. "If this is an indication of the kind of guy he is, then you're better off finding out early." Then Ivory grinned. "Too bad, though, 'cause I know you wanted to give him a little nookie."

Rayanne gently pushed her away as they laughed.

"Come with us," Dorian offered. "We're going to stop by Luanne's shower for half an hour. Afterward, we're going over to the museum for Patti's showing."

Rayanne wanted to go to that showing, but she

was so disappointed with Ralph that she knew she'd be miserable and ruin the day for everyone else.

"No, but I'd like you to take a gift to Luanne for me and tell her I hope she enjoys her shower and I'll call her this week." Rayanne went to her bedroom and returned with the gift. "Tell Patti I'll definitely make the next show," she said.

"Patti will be disappointed," Ivory said. Rayanne smiled weakly.

"We'll see you later," Dorian said.

Dorian and Ivory left and Rayanne was home alone to work, to think. She really liked Ralph and thought he liked her, but what would cause him to behave so selfishly? Oh well, she would never understand what made men tick. Anyway, you win some, you lose some, but life goes on.

Rayanne sent Maxine a birthday card and after talking with her parents and Mrs. Abigail, she typed several pages, then filled her bathtub with water that she added her favorite bath oil to and stepped into the tub. She reclined in the hot scented water, closed her eyes, and just when she'd settled in the silky water and begun to relax, the doorbell rang. It rang a second time before she got out of the tub and slipped on a robe.

If this was Ralph his timing certainly was off, she thought, opening the door. Ralph stood there, holding two dozen roses, one dozen red, one dozen yellow, and he was more handsome than she thought possible.

"I come in peace," he said with a crooked grin on his face.

Rayanne stood back and allowed him to enter.

"These are for you," he said, handing the huge bouquet of roses to her.

"What's with all the roses?" Rayanne asked, and although annoyed, she was glad to see him.

"The yellow ones are to declare our friendship. I don't need to explain the red ones, do I?"

Rayanne closed the door and went to the kitchen to put the flowers in water.

"Am I interrupting something?" Ralph said, following Rayanne into the kitchen.

"I was just taking a bath."

"Where are the others?" he asked, looking around. "Nice place."

"Thanks. Dorian and Ivory are out."

"And you didn't go with them?"

"Don't go there." She looked at him. "You told me you were coming over and I told you I'd be here. Unlike you, I tend to keep my word. I even cooked dinner for you."

"I walked right into that one," Ralph said.

"Why were you so late getting here?"

"I'm sorry, but I got caught up in a hockey game and lost all track of time."

"Next time, call. I'm going to put something on," she said, leaving the room.

Next time, he thought with a smile. That was encouraging.

"And take off that serious face," he said as she entered her room.

When she looked back over her shoulder, she thought she saw a slightly worried look on Ralph's face. *Good,* she thought. *That'll teach him to make me feel all warm and wonderful one moment, then dash cold water on me the next. Well, I can dash a little cold water myself.*

When Rayanne returned, she was wearing a white pantsuit, a pair of tan sandals, and her hair up in a ponytail. Ralph was standing out on the terrace. He turned as he heard her approaching. She was a vision of loveliness, he thought as he stared at her, the delicate features of her face and the tempting curves of her body.

"You look fabulous," he said.

"You're the most complimentary man I've ever met."

"I call 'em as I see 'em," he teased, but Rayanne didn't respond.

Rayanne and Ralph went to SoHo and looked in the windows of some of the art galleries. She hadn't been in that part of the city before, but she liked it. When they went to Chinatown, she was amazed, yet again, at all the wonders that city held.

As they walked along the streets of New York City, Ralph reached over and took Rayanne's hand into his.

"You really cooked dinner for me?" he asked.

Rayanne did not answer him. She simply looked ahead as they continued their journey.

Dorian and Ivory left the shower and took a taxi to the museum. They were greeted by a tall, slender woman, late twenties with long auburn hair, dark features, and startling green eyes.

"Hello, Patti," Dorian said, embracing the woman.

"Hello," Patti said, releasing Dorian and embracing Ivory.

"Good to see you, Patti," Ivory said.

"Yes, I'm glad you both could come," Patti said, her lips curled into a smile. "Is Rayanne here?"

"No, Rayanne was sorry she couldn't be here, but said she would come next time," Ivory informed her.

"This is great, we want to get a closer look at your work," Dorian said.

"You have some wonderful pieces." Ivory looked around. "You've done some great work."

"I'm very excited and," Patti whispered, "there are a number of critics here." Her eyes twinkled.

"I know the showing will be a great success," Dorian said. Ivory nodded in agreement.

A tall older woman waved a slim hand as she approached them. She stopped short and bade Patti to join her. The woman was accompanied by a small dignified-looking man, and the gallery was practically filled with onlookers who wandered around viewing the art pieces.

"Please excuse me a moment," Patti said. "Look around and enjoy the show." Then she whispered, "Wish me luck."

"Good luck, sweetie," Dorian said, and embraced her again. Ivory crossed her fingers and winked at her. Dorian and Ivory admired and appreciated Patti's work.

"Look at this piece," Ivory said of a painting. "She has really captured the passion of this man. Look at those piercing eyes. They seem to reach right out and touch the soul. And that face, there's experience on that face. It's a wonderful piece."

"Uh-huh," Dorian said.

"Which piece do you think we can afford?" Ivory said.

"Ivory, that is so tacky." Dorian grinned.

"Call it what you want, but hell, I want to eat next week and besides, I just worked my ass off getting enough for my portfolio and I don't have a lot of extra, so I can't just walk into an art showing and say wrap it, please."

"Let's just look around a little more. Too bad Rayanne isn't here to help us decide," Dorian said.

Too bad Rayanne isn't here to kick in some of what the piece will cost, Ivory thought.

In the weeks that followed, Ralph and Rayanne spent a lot of time together, becoming more acquainted, and they explored the city every chance they got. They took the subway to Coney Island, rode on the Ferris wheel, the roller coaster, and gouged themselves on everything in sight from hot dogs and french fries to onion rings and popcorn, candy apples and cotton candy, and they washed all those calories down with diet sodas. Ralph took Rayanne shopping at some wonderful shops, they went ice-skating at Rockefeller Center, and they frequented museums. At times, they threw caution to the wind and acted like a couple of kids who were in love for the very first time.

Chapter 7

Dorian had finished that semester and had gone out of town with Henry for a few days, Ivory went to San Francisco to visit friends, and Rayanne stayed behind in New York. She was on her way home from work and had gotten caught in the rain long before she was able to get a taxi. When she arrived at her building, she climbed out of the taxi, splashed in a puddle that had settled in the concrete, and ran into the apartment building.

She opened the door to the loft and the phone rang. She answered it as Sapphire climbed up onto the chair near her. "Ralph?" she said, shaking the water off.

"You all wet?" he asked.

"Yeah. It's coming down in buckets out there." She kicked off her soaked shoes and began removing her wet clothes.

"I know. I just saw you from across the street."

"What are you doing across the street?"

"I was looking for you."

"Well, I'm here, so what are you waiting for?" With that, she hung up the phone.

Rayanne slipped into a robe and hung her wet things across the shower rod in her bathroom.

Ralph arrived and Rayanne let him in. Sapphire took one look at him, gave a weak meow, and escaped from the room.

"Looks like you're all wet also," she said.

"I'm afraid I am."

"Let me get you out of these things," she said, sliding Ralph's coat down his arms. "I can run them down to the dryer or hang them in the bathroom. I'll get you something to cover yourself." She smiled.

Ralph removed the rest of his clothes, wrapped the robe she handed him around him, tying the sleeves around his waist.

"Mind if I light a fire?" he asked.

"No," she called back to him. "There are matches on the mantel."

Ralph lit the fire and lay on the floor in front of it. Rayanne threw Ralph's wet clothes across the rod beside hers. She stood before the mirror in the bathroom and ran a towel over her hair, before braiding the thick long brown locks. When she turned around, Ralph was coming up behind her. She felt herself grow tense, as his body came to rest against her own.

"What's taking you so long? I was lonesome for you," he said.

"Were you?" she said, hoping her voice came out in a normal tone.

"Yes," he said, kissing the back of her neck. "You're shaking. Are you cold?"

"No," she replied, and the single word cracked as it escaped her throat.

She could feel his breath on her neck, the side of

her face. They'd been seeing each other a short while and she'd been comfortable with him, but his closeness now made her weak. He turned her to face him, his arms slid down around her slender waist; then he took her into his arms and kissed her. The kiss was hard at first, almost bruising. When they pulled apart, she saw desire in his eyes that matched exactly what she was feeling. The blood was coursing through her body and instantly she knew she wanted Ralph more than she thought possible. They kissed again and again and when their kisses just weren't enough, Ralph looked at her and whispered, "I'm going to make you my woman."

He pulled her body against his male hardness. His tongue licked over her lips, and she allowed her tongue to play with his. His fingers came up and cupped her breasts and he kissed each of them through the fabric of her robe. When he reached and untied the sash, Rayanne didn't try to stop him, allowing the robe to fall to the floor. He kissed her again, her lips, her throat, and then his lips returned to her nipples. As he nibbled them, she felt the pressure of his teeth connecting with her bare nipples, sending spurts of passion through her body.

Ralph's strong hands roamed over Rayanne's silky smooth body, and in one swift movement, he lifted her up, carried her across the room, and they fell across the bed together. She knew that he was completely aware of how much she delighted in kissing him, having his hands on her, caressing her body freely, how much she was enjoying being with him. It was unbearably thrilling, and she didn't try to conceal her feelings. They kissed and caressed each other until they were overwhelmed with passion. Ralph was completely naked now and Rayanne began placing little kisses on his chest. When Ralph gently slid his hard body into hers and made love to her over and over that night, Rayanne was overwhelmed by a combination of pleasure and pain.

Rayanne awoke the following morning next to Ralph. She opened her eyes and saw him propped on an elbow, looking at her.

"Good morning, beautiful," he said, reveling in the sight of her.

"Good morning," she responded, running her hands over her hair. The braid had come loose during the night and thick locks dangled about her face. "How long have you been awake?" She reached for the covers and drew them close to her neck.

"Not long," he said, admiring her pecan-tan complexion.

Her brown eyes glowed with happiness in her pretty almond-shaped face, as she looked up at him and met his warm gaze. "You should've awakened me."

"I didn't have the heart to disturb Sleeping Beauty." He was unable to take his eyes off her and she wasn't used to having a man beside her when she woke, but Ralph was there and it felt good. He was smiling down at her.

"My God, I must look a mess," she said, trying to move away, but Ralph held her there.

"Where are you going? I want you right here with me," he said. Rayanne looked at him and relaxed in his arms. A warm pleasant feeling enveloped her and at that moment, she knew she cared about this man.

"Baby, making love with you last night was like a pipe dream that I've had all of my adult life. You're the most exciting woman I've ever met. You're wonderful."

"An experienced city man like you finds a little country girl like me exciting, wonderful? That was how you described me, wasn't it?"

"Yes. You are fantastic."

"Fantastic too?" she teased.

"Will you cut it out? Let's suffice it to say that you're the best and now you're my woman. You belong to me."

She liked the sound of possessiveness in his voice.

Later that day Ralph went home, and once he was gone and out of her reach, she missed him. She ached for his presence, his arms around her, his lips on hers, she missed all of him. When Ralph and Rayanne fell in love, it burned like a fire out of control.

The months that followed brought about days of adventure and nights of pleasure. They found that they had a lot in common; they shared a fascination with the same things. Their relationship blossomed, and when Rayanne returned to South Carolina for a brief visit, Ralph accompanied her, and everyone who met Ralph thought her choice was good.

"Oh, damn," Ivory said from her bedroom, rummaging through her drawer. She entered the den with the small box that she'd been keeping her money in. The box was empty. All the money she'd saved the past several months was gone.

They searched all through Ivory's room but they didn't locate the money.

Rayanne asked, "Ivory, are you sure you left the money in your room? You didn't put it into a bank?"

"No. I had it in this box inside the drawer. I took some money for groceries and my trip, but I left the rest in this box. It was there yesterday," Ivory said. "I bet Cal took my money. That idiot spent last night here and he saw me put money in the box. That's why he wasn't here when I woke up this morning. He's never done that before."

Weeks passed and Cal didn't call, nor did he come by. Ivory confessed to the girls that he'd been doing drugs and although she talked about killing Cal when she saw him again and the girls stressed that it was probably for the best that he didn't come back as they would be uncomfortable having a drug user and thief in the house, Ivory didn't appear to share their opinion.

"What more do you want him to do to you, Ivory?" Rayanne asked.

"Rayanne, I don't know why I'm so attracted to Cal. Maybe it's the fact that he's fine or because of the way he makes me feel in bed. I know the man is no good for me, but he's like a drug for me."

"What are you going to do about your portfolio now?" Rayanne asked.

"I'll just have to start from scratch," Ivory said, shaking her head.

The hair that had always hung smooth and silky down Ivory's back was now curly and nappy and clung too close to her head. Rayanne and Dorian noticed it as Ivory rushed past them and into her room. "Ivory," Rayanne called after her, following

Ivory into her bathroom, Dorian on their heels. "Ivory, what happened?"

"Look at this," Ivory screamed, lifting the locks. "Look what that bitch did to my hair."

"What happened?" Dorian asked, touching Ivory's hair. "It feels really rough."

"Hannah put a perm in it. I asked her to use very mild chemicals and not to leave it in too long. Do you think she listened? Hell no." Ivory looked at her hair in the mirror. "Look at this." She lifted a piece of hair and let it fall again. "What the hell am I gonna do now?"

"How long did she keep that stuff in?" Rayanne asked, examining Ivory's hair further.

"I don't know. She kept running all over the place, trying to do all the heads in New York, and when she finally came back to me, it was too late because this is what I got."

"Didn't she use a timer?" Rayanne asked, gently touching Ivory's hair.

"I don't know. Jesus, what am I gonna do? I have a shoot tomorrow, but how can I? I can't go anywhere looking like this," Ivory said. She'd been selected to do a layout for an ad campaign for a cosmetic line, and she'd wanted that job as much as she'd wanted to breathe.

"Your hair always looks so nice, why would you want to have it permed?" Dorian asked.

"I wanted it to look nice for my shoot, so I thought if I had a little curl put in, it would look good. But that's out now. I can't go anywhere looking like this." Ivory lifted her hair and frowned in the mirror at what she saw.

Rayanne looked thoughtful. Her own beautician had performed miracles on her hair, so it was worth a try. "Let me give Elayne a call. She's very good. She may be able to help."

"My hair won't take any more chemicals, Rayanne. I'm just going to have to cut this shit off and hope like hell it grows back," Ivory said, but she loved her hair and cutting it was the last thing she wanted to do. She usually had it trimmed a couple of times a year, but she never really cut it. "They're never gonna hire me looking like this," Ivory said, turning to go to the phone, thinking she'd better call the agency to let them know she couldn't do the job, that they'd have to get someone else.

"Ivory, wait a minute. At least let me call Elayne and see whether she can take a look at your hair before you do anything else," Rayanne said. Ivory lifted both hands in complete exasperation. Rayanne made the call and afterward, they went to the beauty shop.

Elayne took one look at Ivory's hair and said, "Good grief, what happened here? Who did this to you? You musta made somebody mad." She winked at Rayanne. "Oh, gee, all this is gonna have to go. Come sit in my chair." Elayne smiled at Dorian and Rayanne.

Ivory looked back nervously at her friends as she obeyed and sat in the beautician's chair. Elayne sprayed Ivory's hair, pushed her fingers through it, added something from several bottles to saturate the hair from the roots to the ends, then placed a plastic cap on Ivory's head and sat her under the dryer. Ivory's eyes rolled back and forth as the dryer buzzed.

Elayne lifted the head of the dryer, checked Ivory's hair, and pulled it back down onto Ivory's head again. Elayne worked her magic from the shampoo bowl to moisturizers and conditioners, and when she was finished, Ivory's hair hung in beautiful bouncing curls. The girls were so excited with the results that they pooled their money and gave Elayne a ten-dollar tip, with Ivory's promise to return weekly to have her hair treated as well as keeping Elayne as her beautician.

Ivory did the modeling assignment and although she was quite good and she got other calls, she didn't get another job like that for a while. She was faced, once again, with the fact that it was important to have a decent portfolio. Well, she'd have it if even it meant working three jobs because she was still unwilling to borrow the money.

Ivory started seeing Cal again several weeks after the money was stolen and she was reminded by Dorian and Rayanne that she should make Cal return her money. When she didn't, Rayanne wondered what Ivory was using for brains these days.

Rayanne awoke at dawn feeling energized. She was going to make something happen and she was going to begin by getting an agent. She remembered meeting a man named Greg Spriggs at that party at LaVoice's. She'd been impressed by Mr. Spriggs, thought his wife was lovely and friendly, and Rayanne was going to call him today. She had told Mr. Spriggs about her work, her aspirations and interests, and he told her he thought her ideas had potential.

She dialed the number listed on Mr. Spriggs's business card.

When she was put through to him, he said, "Miss Wilson, what can I do for you?"

"Mr. Spriggs, we met at a party at LaVoice's a while ago," she said, knowing he wouldn't remember her. "There were only about five hundred people there that night, so I'm sure you don't remember me."

"Of course I do. You're Rayanne Wilson, the young lady who's written several wonderful plays. You haven't had much success in placing them, but that will change. You've done some acting, but your passion is writing. Am I right so far?" Mr. Spriggs said.

"Yes, I'm that person," Rayanne said, pleased that he'd remembered her.

"I thought you would have called before now. In any event, what can I do for you, Rayanne?"

"Well, Mr. Spriggs—" Rayanne began, but he interrupted.

"Call me Greg, Rayanne. Everyone else around here does."

There was something about Greg Spriggs that made Rayanne feel comfortable, and they made an appointment to meet in three weeks. Greg named a number of clients he represented, and Rayanne felt confident that if anyone could assist her in reaching her goal, it was him.

Rayanne walked out onto the terrace and looked out over the city. Above, the sky was clear and blue and below, the traffic was bumper-to-bumper. She came back in and looked at the clock on the stove. The condo was quiet at six thirty that morning. Ivory and Dorian would be getting up in an hour or so, she thought. Ivory was on the early shift at Jacko's this week, and Dorian had a modeling shoot, but that wasn't until noon. However, she still liked to get up early, get in a good run before the streets got too busy.

The automatic timer on the coffeemaker had already turned itself on and the kitchen smelled of coffee. Rayanne put bread into the toaster and was scrambling eggs when she heard Ivory's shower start up. Minutes later, Ivory grabbed her bag and portfolio with the few good photos she had and rushed toward the front door.

"Where are you off to in such a hurry?" Rayanne asked.

"I've got to be at work a little earlier this morning. I want to put in some extra time because I've got an interview at an agency at ten, but I'll have a sip of that caffeine," Ivory said.

Rayanne handed Ivory a cup that she took a sip from. "I hope this interview materializes into something," Ivory said.

"So do I," Rayanne said. "Are we doing anything tonight?"

"I don't think so, but let me get back with you." Ivory took another sip of coffee and handed the cup back to Rayanne. "See you tonight," she said, rushing out the door.

Chapter 8

"Ivory, are you coming?" Rayanne called out to her. Ivory was always the first to start getting dressed but the last to finish.

"Come on, slowpoke," Dorian said.

"Be there in a sec," Ivory replied, sitting on the foot of her bed with the small box that she kept her money in. She was saving for the portfolio . . . again. She opened the box, took a roll of bills from it, added others to that roll, kissed them, and returned all the bills to the box. She placed the box on the top shelf in her closet for the night, but tomorrow she'd put that money into her bank account where it would be safe until she had enough to get the photos she needed. She would already have had enough for the portfolio had the money not been stolen. But that was a dead issue and she'd never be that careless again.

The show was a barrage of beautifully dressed women gliding up and down a long runway, camera lights flashing, with Ivory wishing she were one of those girls. After the show, they had something to eat and went dancing at a nearby discotheque. When Rayanne returned home that evening, she listened to the single message left on her machine, returned the call to Ralph, removed her makeup, and went to bed.

Rayanne had a full day ahead and was tired, but she was unable to sleep. She had ideas for another play racing around in her head, and the first thing she came up with was the title, which was unusual. Usually, the title didn't come until further along in her stories.

"An Early Awakening," Rayanne whispered into the darkness of her bedroom, and she began to mentally build the story. After storing some thoughts away in her brain, Rayanne felt she could now sleep. Not so, because her mind drifted home to her parents.

She was aware that her father was working too hard and that bothered her. She repeatedly mentioned it to her mother, who expressed concerns as well, but she always said it was Raymond's nature to work hard. Rayanne found that the longer she was away from her parents, the more she missed them. She tossed and turned, but still unable to sleep, she pushed the covers back and got out of bed. She pulled the drapes and looked out the window at a dark and cold New York night, where the fog moved in and hung over the city like a wet blanket. This was a city where everything moved fast and never slept. Although she loved the city, Rayanne couldn't help but wonder what her life would've been like had she not left South Carolina. She was certain it would've been different. Very different.

Rayanne finally dozed off to sleep, but shortly afterward she was awakened by the sound of angry voices. Ivory and Cal were arguing, apparently about money.

"All I need is fifty dollars," he said.

"Get the hell out and get a job," Ivory yelled prior to slamming the door shut.

Rayanne got up and listened, but there wasn't another sound. She went to Ivory's bedroom door and knocked softly.

"Ivory, are you all right?" she asked.

"Yeah, I'm fine, just sleepy," Ivory replied.

Rayanne went into the kitchen to make a cup of herbal tea and she chewed up a Tylenol PM. Tomorrow would be a busy day at the bank and she needed to get some sleep. Sapphire made an entrance and Rayanne picked her up.

"You can't sleep either, huh? Let me get you a little milk. Maybe that will help."

Rayanne poured some milk into a saucer and put Sapphire down to it. She watched as the cat licked up the milk. "You were hungry, weren't you?"

Rayanne left Sapphire with her milk and walked slowly back to her bedroom to wait for the Tylenol to take affect. She crawled back into bed and it wasn't long before she drifted off to sleep again. Sleep was the most precious gift an exhausted mind could give itself, and with working at the bank as well as writing, sleep was the one thing she never seemed to get enough of.

Rayanne awoke, blinking and squinting against the sun that streamed through the windows. She turned away from the sunlight, pulled the covers close, and smiled as she thought of Ralph.

Ralph was the only son of parents who separated when he was a boy. His father raised him and he didn't see his mother again until his freshman year in college. When Ralph told his mother he didn't need her then, she left again and the last he'd heard, she was living somewhere in California. Rayanne found that aside from that, it was amazing how much they had in common, and how completely happy he made her. She sprang out of bed at seven thirty and got dressed for work.

That evening Rayanne typed a couple of short chapters for her new story, then showered, took a container of strawberries from the refrigerator, and ran cold water over them. She poured a cup of coffee. The cabinets were almost bare. There wasn't much left on the shelves in the refrigerator either. It was Ivory's week to buy groceries, but she hadn't. She probably forgot again, as she often had.

Rayanne ate the strawberries and sipped coffee while the air dripped with silence. She was amazed at how well the loft was insulated. The traffic could only be heard when a window or the French doors were opened. Nothing from the outside world could enter unless it was invited. She'd spent the night alone in the loft. Dorian went on a deep-sea fishing trip with friends, and Ivory was in Chicago, compliments of Patti, where her art show was being held.

As Rayanne relaxed and enjoyed the strawberries, she wondered what her mother would say about her eating habits, since Helen had always stressed the importance of having a good breakfast. Rayanne picked up the phone and called home. Everyone was fine. She dialed Greg's number and discussed her new project.

"Sounds good," he said. "It's refreshingly original."

The following day, Rayanne put in a full day at the bank and on her way home, she stopped off at the supermarket to pick up some groceries. Ralph was joining her for dinner and she'd make the cabbage and sausage dish he loved so much. She also picked up a bunch of cut flowers. She put the milk, meat, and eggs in the refrigerator, and she put the flowers in water before rushing out again, this time to shop for bathing suits. Ralph was taking her on a trip where they would bask in the sun, was all he'd said. He was an intriguing man.

Chapter 9

On a great cloudless day in late November, Ralph and Rayanne walked along the beach hand in hand, in beautiful San Juan. The temperatures were in the eighties, unlike temperatures they had left in New York five hours earlier when they had boarded the flight. The flight brought them to a warm, sunny, tropical paradise, where they would spend five glorious days, engaging in wonderful daily activities and nights of dining and dancing.

Puerto Rico is a top Caribbean destination because of the easy air access from the U.S., and although Ralph had visited other cities in the Caribbean, San Juan was his favorite and he was certain it would be Rayanne's as well.

They checked in at the Condado Plaza Hotel and Casino, which offered fabulous dining that would satisfy the varying tastes of people around the world. San Juan offers a tourist vast excitement. The nightlife alone is considered to be legendary. They enjoyed Las Vegas–type shows, late night casino action, and discotheques, where popular American songs drifted through the air for listening and dancing pleasures. Since Puerto Rico is a United States Commonwealth, the currency is the dollar, and Americans can enter the island without the necessity of visas or passports, and they can spend the American dollar all day, every day.

Rayanne and Ralph enjoyed beautiful white sand beaches with water so clear the coral reefs were visible. They walked along a secluded part of the beach, and Ralph lifted Rayanne up over his shoulders and carried her out into the ocean.

They explored the coves and nooks and gathered seashells. They stopped off at a nearby restaurant and gulped their food with an urgency to return to the beach. They were approached by a representative for one of the hotels that offered a time-sharing tour scheduled for the following day.

Puerto Rico was unlike any place Rayanne had ever experienced. They ventured out until the water washed up against their ankles, and white foam ran through their toes.

"This is a wonderful surprise, honey," Rayanne said, taking a deep breath.

"I'm glad you like it. There is so much more that I want to show you."

They stood together, listening to the surf and watching the waves lick at the sand as the tide rolled in and out. Rayanne felt as though she was drifting, being carried away by the ocean.

They entered the dining room that evening to the soft murmur of people talking, music playing, and beautifully dressed people walking around the vast chandeliered room. The maitre d' greeted them and led them to a secluded table near a low open window where they could hear the ocean slapping against the large rocks. It had started to rain and the lights and the moon caused the raindrops to resemble diamonds falling from heaven to merge with the surf. The moon was serene and high in the sky, casting a silver reflection on the ocean.

They ordered and fell silent and the only sound was the lapping of the waves. The waiter brought them a tall concoction each with a tiny umbrella.

"These look fabulous," Rayanne said before sipping her drink.

"They are. This place has changed a lot since I was here six years ago."

"Six years is a long time, and I'm sure the changes are for the better."

"On all counts," he said.

The salad and shrimp cocktails arrived.

Although Rayanne and Ralph talked and shared a lot, she knew there were still things he kept private. "You don't like talking much about your past, do you?"

"I suppose there are some things that should be left in the dark and forgotten past."

Rayanne looked into his eyes. One of the things she liked most about their relationship was the sharing, but she knew there was still so much he kept to himself.

Ralph looked at her and took a deep breath. "I brought my wife here on our honeymoon. Later when problems came up in our marriage, since we'd liked this place so much, we came back on our fifth anniversary, a second honeymoon, hoping to recapture what we had. This was a place of magic for us, but our last two years together, we were going in different directions," he explained.

"I don't suppose it helped much, coming back here, I mean," Rayanne said.

"I don't suppose it did because as it turned out,

she got pregnant right here as near as we could figure it. She miscarried in her sixth month and within a year, we were divorced."

Ralph's eyes wandered out to the ocean. Rayanne felt his agony and his loss and even though she wanted to comfort him, make him forget the past, she had no words for him. He looked at her.

"Rayanne, I didn't bring you here for any reason other than the fact that I love this place and I love you and I want to associate this place with wonderful memories. Please believe that."

"I do," Rayanne said. "I'm just sorry it couldn't hold all happy memories for you."

"Don't be. We had some great times, but we realized it wasn't meant to be."

Ralph explained that after the divorce, his former wife moved back to Massachusetts to be near her parents. They spoke occasionally by phone but didn't see much of each other after the move. Ralph had gone through so much in his life. He'd divorced after seven years of marriage and he later fell in love with another woman. They had a child but they both died in a freak auto accident. If anyone had experienced bad luck, it was Ralph, but Rayanne hoped his future would be brighter, and she would do what she could to help. She was surprised, though, that when Ralph spoke again, his voice didn't appear to ring of any remorse.

After dinner they moved into the lounge and enjoyed the singer performing some of their favorite tunes. They danced and stole kisses while on the dance floor.

"Have I told you how much I'm enjoying being here with you?" she said, running her arms up around his neck.

"Yes, but you can tell me as often as you'd like." He smiled into her eyes.

"When you look at me that way, you put me in such a warm, vulnerable frame of mind."

When the song ended, he whispered in her ear, "Let's go."

They walked along the beach before turning in and there was little evidence that it had rained earlier. Rayanne kicked off her shoes and ran across the sand toward the water. Ralph threw his jacket to the ground, took off one shoe, danced on one foot, and alternated until he too was barefoot. He rolled up his pant legs and ran after her. She looked back, saw him coming, and ran directly into the ocean. When he caught up with her, he kissed her softly and tenderly and there in the moonlight, they created an evening they'd remember even in old age.

Just as the sun began to rise and daylight faded the darkness of night, Rayanne awoke nestled in Ralph's arms. He was opening doors within her that allowed her to do things she never thought possible. Ralph woke up. "Good morning, gorgeous," he said.

"Morning yourself, big guy," she replied, and they held each other and enjoyed the quiet for a while before getting up. Later they swam in the hotel pool, shopped along the strip, purchasing souvenirs for their friends, and at twelve thirty they were met in their hotel lobby by the time-sharing representative for another hotel. They toured a hotel, had lunch, and were driven to Old San Juan, where they walked on the cobblestone streets.

Old San Juan offered sophisticated and up-to-date conveniences where someone could go back in time viewing the Spanish Colonial buildings with balconies dating from the seventeenth and eighteenth centuries. Many of the buildings housed superb restaurants, craft shops, boutiques, galleries, and museums, which they wanted to see again before leaving Puerto Rico.

They rode back to the El San Juan Hotel and Casino, where they watched the film and toured the rooms and suites of the finest decor. Ralph didn't buy into the plan, but he took the literature and promised he'd give it some thought.

They spent their days enjoying the beaches, sightseeing, and countless other things, but as with anything good, the time was passing much too quickly.

Rayanne awoke early the day before their departure. She leaned over and kissed a sleeping Ralph before easing out of bed. She called her parents to let them know that they would return to New York the following day. Then she called Greg. Afterward she walked out onto the private balcony and gazed out at a beautiful stretch of beaches and she watched the palm trees swaying and dancing to the silent tune of the early morning breezes. The ocean with its timeless waves moved in and out, and the waters were divided; one half of the ocean was blue, the other, green.

Rayanne quietly put on a shorts set over a bikini, pulled her hair up into a ponytail, and left the room. She pulled off her sandals and walked along the edge of the water, enjoying the sun on her face and the soothing sounds of the ocean. Then she began to run and as she did, she peeled off her shorts and top, flung them to the ground, and dove into the water. After enjoying the water for more than an hour, Rayanne gathered her things and began walking slowly back toward the hotel, when she saw Ralph's tall masculine body approaching her.

"You finally woke up," Rayanne teased. "I wanted to come out before it got too crowded and you were sleeping so peacefully, I didn't want to disturb you."

"Baby, next time, disturb me. Weren't you a little intimidated coming out here alone, dressed like that?" he asked, eyeing her.

"There's nothing wrong with a little fear in your life every once in a while. Makes you feel alive," she teased.

"Oh, you are alive. You can prove that by me."

"Tomorrow, we'll leave all this behind," Rayanne said, looking around. "But it has been wonderful."

"It doesn't have to end tomorrow. We can stay a little longer if you want."

"I'd love to, honey, but I suppose we'd better get back to the real world. I have a couple of meetings scheduled for Friday."

"I thought you said you had one meeting," Ralph said, raising one finger.

"I did but I called Greg to run something by him, and he wants to meet with me also, but aside from that, I promised Ivory and Dorian that I'd go to the Knicks game with them."

"I thought they were both away."

"Yeah, but they'll be back by then."

"My baby is definitely a New York Knickerbocker fan," he said, and smiled at her. "Happy?"

"I'm ecstatic," she replied. "What about you?"

"I've never been happier. What did I do to deserve you?"

"You were just born lucky, I guess," she said, and smiled.

Ralph looked at Rayanne a moment. "Tell me something. If you had one wish, what would it be?"

"You can't just give me one wish. You have to give me at least two."

"Okay, if you had two wishes, then."

"Family and friends, health and happiness outweighing everything else, I'd wish for the love of the man of my dreams, and a hit play."

"You've got me," he said.

"I know that, but I get two wishes, remember, and I want both. In fact, I want it all," she said, and smiled wickedly at him.

"And you'll have it. It takes time, but it'll happen."

"If there's anything that I'm certain about, it is that I'm going to have a successful writing career."

Ralph drove their rented car to Old San Juan, where they shopped and took snapshots of the French Colonial architecture. They observed the largest cruise ship ports, sneaked into one of the ocean liners, and giggled like two children at their success. Then they were off to a variety of cultural festivities that punctuated San Juan, and it was evident to Ralph that the island was working hard at improving its tourism product.

Later, they took shots of the lush rain forest, the waterfalls, wild orchids, ferns, and towering palm trees. Afterward, they drove back to the hotel, ate lunch, and walked on the beach.

The sun had moved across the sky and stopped just long enough to meet the ocean and cast a fiery path reflecting across the waters, extending from the west to where their feet were planted in the sand, before it suddenly sank and vanished.

That night they visited the casino and before going back to their room to pack, they took a final walk on the beach.

The next morning they rode most of the way back to the airport in silence. They purchased a collar for Sapphire and as the plane climbed away from the island, Rayanne was sad leaving the tropical paradise behind.

Chapter 10

After jogging an hour, Ivory and Rayanne entered the loft wearing sweat suits, and headed to the refrigerator for bottles of water. Although Rayanne had moved into a permanent position at the bank, she continued to write and waited for that big break.

"Sooner or later, something's gotta happen," she told Ivory, removing the towel from her neck and flopping down onto the couch.

"It's just a matter of time, girl," Ivory said, taking a sip of water.

Rayanne handed Ivory a section of the newspaper. "Gosh," Rayanne said.

Ivory looked over at her. "What?"

"Every time I open the paper or watch the news, all I see is crime. Some man beat up his wife and his son because they drank all the milk," Rayanne said. "Can you believe that?"

"These people are crazy," Ivory said.

"What is this world coming to?"

"I don't think it's gonna get any better."

"I wish people would wake up and live," Rayanne

said sadly. "It makes you wonder what the next ten years will bring."

"What about tomorrow? I'm afraid of what might happen to change our lives within the next twenty-four hours."

Ivory tossed the paper on the coffee table and picked up a magazine. After studying the face of the girl who was on the cover she said, "This is gonna be me one day."

"Your face is gonna be on many covers one day. Ivory, you know it's gonna happen. We're gonna be rich, successful career women," Rayanne said, and asked, "How is it going with your new job?"

"It's okay. At least I've got medical and dental coverage. I haven't recovered financially since I had that surgery when I was working part-time and the company didn't provide insurance coverage. My eyes are open now, I bet," Ivory said. "In order to get some real benefits, I need a real job."

Ivory had applied for a job in an accounting firm and was hired. The job was working out and she felt better knowing she had insurance coverage and she hoped never to be in a position of not have coverage again even if she didn't have enough money left to buy a pack of cigarettes, she'd told Rayanne and Dorian.

"Did I tell you what happened today? You remember Yolanda?"

"Your receptionist?"

"Yeah. She's been with us about six months," Ivory answered. "Well, when I got my income tax return, she asked me to loan her six hundred with the promise that she'd pay back eight hundred."

"That's what happened to all that money you got?" Rayanne asked, remembering that Ivory had gotten a large income tax return that year and she'd advised Ivory that it wasn't a good idea to lend that kind of money to someone she barely knew. Ivory had made the loan anyway.

"Yolanda was to pay me a hundred dollars a pay period, two hundred a month until the debt was paid, but that bitch quit her job a week ago," Ivory relayed.

"Oh no," Rayanne said. "What about your money?"

"Wait a minute." Ivory paused a minute to turn the page of the magazine. Rayanne wondered whether she was going to finish this story and if it would be that night. "Yolanda quit a week ago. Wait, I'm getting a little ahead of myself. She actually resigned over a week ago, but because my boss had been sick and we hadn't found a replacement for Yolanda, she agreed to work three more weeks. Well, she paid me a hundred dollars a pay period as scheduled until she'd paid three hundred. Yesterday she gave me two postdated checks, one to be cashed today for a hundred, and one for two hundred two weeks from today."

"Okay, okay," Rayanne said. "So you will be getting your money back."

"I sometimes have lunch with the payroll clerk and he told me that Yolanda gave him a form to terminate her direct deposit. Well, I cashed her first check when I was on the way to work this morning, figuring in two weeks, I'd cash the last check."

"So you won't be getting all of your money back since Yolanda had terminated her direct deposit."

"I wouldn't, but Payroll told me that she owed others and was going to give all of us the shaft, but guess what I did?" Ivory said.

"Lord, I can't imagine, but do tell." Rayanne's curiosity was piqued.

"I changed the date on the last check and I went right back to the bank and cashed the second check."

"You did?" Rayanne squealed.

"You're damn right I did. Payroll is holding the change for a few days. Then they'd have to put it through and after that, she'd be getting her check in her hand. In the meantime, I would've been holding a two-hundred-dollar check on a closed account or an account with insufficient funds."

"You cashed the second check," Rayanne said. "This is too good."

"Isn't it, though?" Ivory said.

"You little devil, but, girl, that was a good move."

"That hoochie was gonna return to L.A. without paying me my damn two-hundred-dollars."

"You're too much," Rayanne said with delight.

"Of course." Ivory laughed. "I've got my money but when she's hit with all those returned check charges, she'll know not to fuck with me and I don't care about the $200 interest. It probably wasn't legal anyway."

"Girl, you're so crazy," Rayanne said, and they laughed, but their gaiety was short-lived and they were startled when they heard the entrance door slam shut and the sound of Dorian crying.

"Damn him," she said tearfully.

Rayanne got up and rushed over to Dorian with Ivory closely behind her.

"Dorian, what's wrong?" Rayanne asked as she and Ivory led Dorian to the couch.

"Henry and I had an argument. He wants to end the relationship. I'm too demanding, he says,"

Dorian shared. "He thinks I'm taking him away from his home and work too much."

"Why, that son of a bitch," Ivory said. "Did you tell him you were not trying to hear that shit?"

Ivory couldn't believe it. After all, wasn't it Henry who was supposed to be getting a divorce and he was the one who was always calling Dorian, trying to control her life?

"I'll bet he is getting grief from Olympia," Rayanne said. "Dorian, get rid of the guy. Don't let him do this to you."

"He doesn't always act like this. Sometimes he acts as though he can't live without me, then this," Dorian said, looking hurt and confused.

Then the doorbell rang and Ivory answered it.

"What's up, Henry?" she asked coolly, staring him in his eyes.

"I'd like to see Dorian, please," he said, wringing his hands together.

"I don't think she wants to see you," Ivory said with an attitude.

"Please, I just need to see Dorian for a few minutes."

"What did you do to her?" Ivory scolded.

"I didn't handle things very well. That's why I need to talk to her. Please," he begged.

Dorian appeared and Rayanne was on her heels.

"Dorian, do you want to see this man?" Ivory asked.

"It's okay," Dorian said.

"Are you sure?" Rayanne asked, a hand on Dorian's shoulder.

Dorian nodded affirmatively.

"Let us know if you need us," Rayanne said, and

she and Ivory left the foyer with Ivory giving Henry a look.

When Henry and Dorian were alone, he said, "I was afraid you wouldn't see me."

"Why are you here, Henry?"

"I didn't want to leave things the way they were between us."

"Henry, you told me you want to end the relationship. How am I supposed to feel?"

"I didn't mean that. It came out all wrong."

"How many ways can you say that you don't want to see me anymore?"

She headed for the living room with Henry following her.

"I do want to see you," he said sullenly.

"Well then, what the hell were you trying to say to me?"

"I don't know what I'm doing anymore. All I know is that when you left me back there I felt like my world was coming apart."

"I don't know what you want from me. You keep telling me you're getting a divorce and we are going to get married. That hasn't happened. It appears you want me in your life but you don't know what to do with me."

"That's not it at all. I love you, Dorian. I just need time."

"I have given you time, years even, and still nothing."

"Just give me a little more time and don't stop loving me," he said.

"You want me to put my life on hold until you decide what you want to do with yours. Do you think that's fair?"

"I don't want to lose you."

"You don't want to lose Olympia either," she said.

"Yes, but what I feel for her is nothing compared to what I feel for you." Henry smoothed his hair back. "I want you." He paused a moment. "In all the time that we've been seeing each other, we've never had a serious argument. I guess I took it for granted that you'd always be there for me in whatever capacity I needed, but I was wrong, and it didn't occur to me until you said good-bye just how wrong I was."

"I am not going to put my life on hold and wait for you to make an honest woman out of me. To hell with that," she spat out.

"Soon, sweetheart, soon," he said.

"Henry, this is not going to be all about what you want. I can't do this anymore."

"Baby, just be patient. I will never take you for granted again, and I will always be there for you," Henry said, and when he left, Dorian was left with the promise of hope for a future for them.

In the months that followed, Henry did spend more time with Dorian and Rayanne, and Ivory thought that maybe Henry was going to move that divorce along and marry Dorian.

"Damn," Ivory said. "This yeast infection is driving me crazy."

"Have you seen a doctor?" Rayanne asked.

"Not yet."

"What are you waiting for?" Dorian asked.

"I've got some of that vaginal cream left," Rayanne said, "but I don't have an applicator."

"Hand that cream over. I think I've got an applicator," Ivory said.

Rayanne went into her room, and returned with a tube that she handed to Ivory. "If it's a simple yeast infection, this should work," Rayanne said. "But you should still see a doctor."

"Not if this works," Ivory said. "Hey, I want to show y'all my portfolio."

"You got the pictures?" Dorian asked excitedly.

Ivory went to her room and returned with her portfolio. She sat between the girls and began to slowly flip the pages.

"Oooh, Ivory, these are great," Rayanne said.

"Yeeaah," Dorian agreed.

"I'm pleased with them. Beginning Monday morning, I'm gonna hit all the top modeling agencies in New York and see what happens," Ivory said.

Both girls had done some modeling, and although Dorian had gotten far more assignments than Ivory, their success wasn't yet as great as either had hoped.

When they finished looking at the photos, Ivory put the portfolio on the coffee table.

"Hey, y'all," Ivory said. "Let's go home this weekend."

"That'll be great," Dorian said.

"What are we going to do for money?" Rayanne asked.

"We'll charge it," Ivory said. "What do you say?"

Rayanne considered for a moment, then lifting her shoulders said, "Sure, that'll work." Ivory still could talk her into just about anything. "Should we call and let our folks know we're coming?" she asked.

"Why don't we surprise them?" Ivory suggested.

"That'll work too," Rayanne said.

They took a flight on Friday evening, and Rayanne's and Ivory's parents were surprised, but as always, they were happy when the girls came home. After visiting their families, Aunt Bessie, and Mrs. Abigail, on Saturday night the girls went to a nightclub to hear a popular group perform.

"Who is that girl?" Ivory asked.

"Someone said she is local," Rayanne said.

"She has a dynamite voice," Dorian said. "She's going places."

They enjoyed the first set and afterward they stood and waited in a long line to the ladies' room. When they returned to their table, they ordered more drinks, danced between shows, and enjoyed the last set.

Late Sunday night, they returned to New York and Ivory took her portfolio to work and did a lot of interviews before work or on her lunch hour.

Dorian was one of a couple of dozen models who'd been interviewed for a shoot in Europe. She was excited because she was one of the models that was asked to come back.

Dorian got the assignment and went to Europe, Rayanne's writing was improving, and Ivory got the promotion in the accounting firm where she worked and she was happy about that, but her supposed yeast infection turned out to be an STD and she was pissed. Ivory vowed never to see Cal again. Rayanne was sorry about her reasoning for not allowing Cal to come back to the loft, but she was grateful that he was out of their lives, so she thought.

Rayanne was awakened just before daybreak to a persistent knock at her door. Since Cal had become a constant overnight guest again, Rayanne had begun locking her door before going to bed and sometimes out of habit, she still did. Cal was a drug user and a thief, and a combination like that was unpredictable.

The knocking continued. At first, Rayanne thought she was dreaming. She'd been sleeping soundly from the sleeping pill she'd taken before going to bed and, dazed, she got up and opened the door. Ivory was standing there in her nightgown, looking frightened.

"Ivory, what's wrong?"

"Something is wrong with Cal," Ivory said.

"Cal is here?" Rayanne blinked.

"Yeah."

"Ivory, you said you were not going to let him come back here anymore."

"I think Cal is dead."

"He can't be."

"I shook him but he didn't respond," Ivory said as her voice quavered.

Dorian joined them at Rayanne's door.

"What's going on?" Dorian asked.

"Ivory said Cal is dead," Rayanne said nervously, going toward Ivory's room.

"Cal is dead?" Dorian said. "Cal is dead?" she repeated, following Rayanne and Ivory.

The three girls walked up to Ivory's bed. Rayanne reached down and touched Cal's pulse. "I believe he is dead," she said.

"Oh no." Ivory began to cry.

"Oh my God," Dorian said, her hands going up to her mouth.

"What am I gonna do?" Ivory was becoming hysterical.

"Ivory, we have got to call the police," Rayanne said.

"I'm afraid to call the police. What if they think I did something to him?" Ivory said.

"Why would they think that?" Rayanne asked. "Ivory, what happened?"

"Nothing, I don't know. Nothing really. When Cal came over tonight, I gave him a hard time about giving me that STD, but that's all," Ivory stuttered through her reply.

"Did he seem all right when he came?" Rayanne asked.

Ivory lowered her head. "I saw him coming out of the bathroom with a needle and some other things in a plastic bag," she said. "Then he wanted to go to bed, but I wouldn't let him. That's why he still has all his clothes on."

"Dorian, please call the police," Rayanne said.

"Let's call his father. He is a policeman," Ivory said.

"Do you have a number for him, Ivory?" Dorian asked.

Ivory went through Cal's wallet, located a number, and Rayanne placed the call.

Rayanne and Dorian walked with Ivory back out to the couch and they waited for Cal's father to get there. Ivory started crying again and Rayanne and Dorian tried to calm her down.

Cal's father came over, examined his son's body, and called for an ambulance. With them came more police.

It appeared he'd died of a drug overdose. Cal had been using drugs for years; Cal's father informed them he was aware of his son's drug use, but as is with many parents, he couldn't force his son to quit or get help. Cal had kept his drug use a secret for some time, mostly because he injected the drugs under his toenails, which left no visible marks on his body.

Because of the position Cal's father held with the police department, there was limited publicity. Neither Rayanne nor Dorian cared much for Cal, mainly because of the way he treated Ivory, but they certainly didn't want to see him dead.

Cal's father came to the loft once more after that night. He wanted to know whether Cal was upset. Captain Braverman even asked if Ivory knew where Cal was getting the drugs. Since they didn't hear anything further, it appeared the matter was resolved.

Ivory changed after Cal's death. She didn't joke around as she once did, she didn't go out much with the girls, and she didn't date. She went on interviews and began landing one modeling job after the other. Since she wanted to keep busy, she kept her job at the bank for a couple of months but was forced to quit because she was so busy with modeling assignments.

Dorian quit her side job and she devoted herself full-time to modeling and both Ivory and Dorian were out of town more than they were at home.

Chapter 11

Rayanne's wish to have a hit play came not a moment too soon. She felt she'd waited a lifetime to realize her dream, but it was finally here.

She'd just celebrated her twenty-third birthday two weeks ago when Greg called her.

"Rayanne," he said. "Are you sitting down?"

"Yes, Greg. Why? What's up?" Rayanne asked.

"I think we've found a buyer for your play."

"What?" she asked excitedly.

"We've got some people who are showing interest in, *Papa, Come Home*," he said. That was the last play she'd written. She'd written several that Greg shopped for her, but they went absolutely nowhere, fast.

"What exactly does that mean?"

"It means someone wants to buy your play."

"I don't believe it."

"Well, it's true."

Rayanne wasn't sure what to say, but she knew this was a big step in a writer's career and now that her dream was materializing, she was speechless.

"We need to get together and look over the

contract and if you are satisfied, you can sign on the dotted line and we'll be in business. Are you interested?" he asked.

Greg and Rayanne made an appointment and when they hung up, she called her parents and shared her good news, with them expressing joy for their daughter, knowing she'd worked hard to make her dream come true. When Rayanne hung up from them, she pulled her feet up on the couch, hugged her knees, and thanked God.

On opening night, the thunderous applause gave Rayanne every indication that the play was a hit, and as if that wasn't enough, the reviews the following morning were phenomenal. That was Rayanne's first big break. In the midst of her excitement, she was ecstatic at the number of family members and friends from back home who came to see the play on opening night.

The play quickly moved from Off Broadway to Broadway, and when they held her first reception, the champagne flowed, people were moving around, and Rayanne was trying hard to relax. She was so nervous. She shook hundreds of hands, made small talk with numerous people, and smiled until she thought her face would crack.

Ralph had promised to be at Rayanne's side that evening, but shortly after they entered the reception hall, he began wandering around. She was relieved when he crept up behind her and whispered, "Meet me in the powder room."

She entered the powder room and Ralph took her hand and pulled her into a private area, where he introduced her to her first date with marijuana.

Minutes after she'd inhaled from the joint he'd lit and passed on to her, she returned to the ballroom where she mingled, danced, told jokes, and became the life of the party.

Soon after that night, Rayanne quit her job at the bank and began to write full-time. The second play she wrote was picked up, but she didn't get great reviews and it ended after a very short run. However, the first play was moving around the country.

Dorian and Ivory were busy and were doing interesting things with their lives as well. They skied in Aspen, spent weekends in Atlantic City, dined in the most exclusive restaurants, traveled extensively. After a while, they even hired a housekeeper.

When Greg found a buyer for an additional play, Rayanne began looking into purchasing real estate. All three girls had worked hard for years. They experienced highs and lows. But after they'd struggled for so long, it appeared now that they'd made it.

Ivory seemed to have put men on hold since the incident with Cal. She went out but she did not bring anyone home with her or allow anyone to stay overnight. Ivory threw herself into her work. She landed a huge job as a parts model where she earned as much as ten thousand dollars a day just to model her hands for several hours a day. When she tested for a feet advertisement, she recommended Dorian, who was brought in, tested, and signed to do her feet, legs, and several cosmetics ads. Each of them did numerous TV commercials and layouts for magazines, and they received modeling jobs that took them across the U.S.A. and abroad. And, as Ivory had always wanted, her picture was on the cover of every major magazine in the country, and she bought dozens of copies and sent them to people she knew back home.

Dorian had finished graduate school, and she was on top of the world in the modeling industry, so much so that she was able to choose the assignments she wanted. And when it came to magazine covers, she was on a cover one month and Ivory was on that cover the next month, and vice versa.

It wasn't long before Rayanne became one of the youngest and most successful playwrights in New York City. She'd become the person she wanted to be, and she was counting her blessings and Ralph was a wonderful addition in those blessings. He was supportive and encouraging, and Rayanne was convinced that she'd marry Ralph one day. They'd talked about marriage, but she'd made it clear about the things she wanted to accomplish before getting married, and Ralph understood.

Chapter 12

Returning to the loft after seeing *Die Fledermaus* at the Met, Rayanne and Ralph, Dorian, Henry and Ivory, who had begun dating again, and Eric ate the meal Gertie, their housekeeper, had prepared for them. There were no further words on Henry's divorce and no one mentioned it anymore.

Rayanne had a small chunk of lobster on the tip of her fork and she fed it to Ralph. When dinner was over and the girls were left alone, Ivory blew out the candles and they cleared the table. "Did you see my girl feeding Ralph from her fork?" Ivory asked.

"I certainly did," Dorian replied.

"Those guys are really in love," Ivory said.

"He's a very nice man," Rayanne said, piling dishes into the sink and filling it with water. Although there was a dishwasher, Rayanne sometimes insisted on doing the dishes by hand. She said it kept her grounded. Dorian said she never understood that because Rayanne was one of the most down-to-earth, grounded persons she knew.

"Why don't we just let the dishwasher do the work while we talk?" Ivory asked.

"I don't mind doing them sometimes. You guys just sit and talk with me," Rayanne said.

"I just had my nails done so I'm not going to soak my hands in dishwater," Ivory laughed.

"I said just keep me company," Rayanne said.

"We may as well pitch in and help or we won't ever hear the last of it," Dorian said, and they laughed.

"So, things are going well for you and Ralph," Dorian said.

"Yeah, he is very understanding of my time to write and I appreciate that, but we do spend our spare time with each other," Rayanne said.

"Eric is nice, I like him, but nothing serious," Ivory said, and although she'd not found the man she wanted to spend the rest of her life with, she was happy that Rayanne had found the man of her dreams.

"You'll find that right someone one day," Rayanne said.

She'd gone out with other men on occasions since meeting Ralph, though those dates were casual and strictly platonic, but now she wasn't interested in seeing anyone else in any capacity.

"So, what have you guys been doing? You are seldom around. I don't see you anymore. If you two aren't on a plane to Milan, you're jet-setting to Paris. I believe the two of you are in Europe more than you are here," Rayanne teased.

"Are you two thinking of getting married?" Dorian asked, and there was something in her voice that gave Ivory and Rayanne pause.

"What? No. Well, at some point, but I'm not going to rush out tomorrow and do it, though I think it's getting close. What about you guys?" Rayanne asked.

"Perhaps, we're just not ready. Have you thought of that?" Dorian snapped, which took Ivory and Rayanne by surprise. With Rayanne's and Ivory's mouths hanging open, Dorian continued. "Just because you choose to sleep with one man doesn't mean that everyone else has to. It's a matter of choice."

Rayanne looked at Dorian, then at Ivory. "I don't get it." Rayanne lifted her hand, baffled by Dorian's unusual outburst.

"How you live your life is your business, but don't expect everyone else to do it," Dorian said.

"Dorian, what are you talking about? All I was saying is that in the not too distant future, Ralph and I will probably get married," Rayanne said, handing a plate she'd washed to Ivory.

"You can do it tomorrow for all I care," Dorian said, sarcastically and totally unexpectedly.

"Dorian, what's going on?" Rayanne asked, holding an unwashed cup in her hand. "Is everything all right with you?" She'd noticed that the last couple of times that they'd seen each other, Dorian didn't seem her old self.

"Everything's fine."

"And Henry?" Rayanne asked, continuing to do the dishes.

"I don't want to get into anything about Henry tonight," Dorian snapped, slamming a stack of plates on the counter and rushing from the kitchen to the den.

"Dorian, what's wrong?" Rayanne asked, dropping the dishcloth into the sink and following Dorian.

"I said I don't want to talk about it," Dorian said, her eyes flashing with anger.

"I just want you to be happy," Rayanne said, walking over to Dorian.

"I'm happy and why wouldn't I be? I have everything anyone could want," Dorian said.

"Okay," Rayanne said, lifting her hands and going to sit in a chair across the room, "but let me know if I can do anything."

"I've told you I'm fine," Dorian said, turning away from the window. "Just because you've allowed your life to become one-dimensional, don't think that I'm going to. You'd probably be a lot happier if you do as I do."

"Oh?" Rayanne said, turning to stare at Dorian.

Ivory, observing from the kitchen, said, "Knock it off, you guys." Rayanne and Dorian had had disagreements before, but never like this.

"You would probably be a lot happier if you played the field," Dorian said, ignoring Ivory.

"Is there something you want to tell me?" Rayanne asked.

"No, you keep living with your head in the sand and give your heart to one man," Dorian said sarcastically.

"And you choose to be stuck in a dead-end situation that isn't going anywhere," Rayanne said.

"Will you two cut this shit out?" Ivory said, getting between the two girls, not liking the direction where the conversation was heading.

Dorian looked at Rayanne, her lips began to quiver, and then she stormed out of the room.

"Good Lord, what's going on here?" Rayanne said, annoyed that she lost control and hadn't handled the situation better.

"She'll be okay," Ivory said, putting the dishcloth near the sink, and went to check on Dorian.

When Ivory returned, Rayanne said, "Is she okay?"

"She's all right," Ivory said.

"Ivory, is there something going on here that I don't know about?" Rayanne asked, following Ivory back into the kitchen.

"Rayanne, some of the things I'm about to tell you," Ivory began, "I learned by accident."

"Were you snooping again?" Rayanne asked, knowing that no secret was safe from Ivory.

"Of course. Some time ago, I came across some old photographs in Dorian's room. There were pictures of a little girl, six or seven years old, and a man and woman. Dorian and her parents, I believe. When I asked her about the people in the pictures, she refused to talk about them, telling me to mind my own business, and I never brought that subject up again. Neither has she," Ivory said, and there was a pause. Rayanne walked over to the sink where Ivory was.

"So, what's the point?" Rayanne asked, not knowing what Ivory was getting at.

"When I first saw the pictures, the man looked strangely familiar, but I couldn't put it together. The man in the photographs looks exactly like Henry, except Henry looks a little younger. So, are you thinking what I'm thinking?" Ivory asked.

"That Henry represents some sort of father figure for Dorian," Rayanne said.

Dorian was a sweet, loving person, but she never talked about her parents, which Rayanne thought was odd. Did they have a falling-out and weren't able to reconcile their differences? Did Dorian's parents know where she was, whether she was even alive? Dorian's face had been plastered on magazine covers around the world; why hadn't her parents tried to contact her?

Rayanne's own family was close and she had no idea what it would be like not to be in contact with her relatives. Her sister Lila was the most taxing person in her family, but even she deserved that bonding with her family.

"That's my guess," Ivory was saying.

"Where did you see the pictures?" Rayanne asked, her mind at work. Maybe she could find something that would help them learn more about Dorian. As it was, they didn't know a lot. Anytime they asked about Dorian's personal life, she'd either become quiet, say she didn't want to talk about it, or just change the subject.

"It doesn't matter. The pictures are no longer there," Ivory said.

"You tried to get another look at them, didn't you?"

"Yes, but only because I thought I could learn something about her. There were some clippings too," Ivory said, "but I didn't get a chance to read any of them."

"There must be something very painful in her past, and since she's never talked about her folks, it makes you wonder." Then Rayanne was struck by an idea. "Do you think Dorian's folks gave her up for adoption? That might explain some of the bitterness and the secrecy."

"Anything's possible. All I know is that she's going through a lot right now. You know she's always said that you and I are the only real family she's got, and I believe she really feels that way too. I wouldn't be a bit surprised if she's behaving this way because you're moving out and she thinks our little family is breaking up."

"That's ridiculous," Rayanne said. "We'll see each other just as often as we do now, we'll just be living in different places. Nothing else will change. Dorian must know that."

"You'd think so," Ivory said, putting up the last dish. "I'm gonna miss not having you here also, but I'll know how to reach you." They moved back into the den. Ivory sat and propped her feet up on the coffee table. "I've thought of buying a house myself. The loft is nice, but I want something of my own eventually. I need to be here for Dorian a while to see what her plans are."

"You do think she is all right, though?" Rayanne asked.

"She just needs to understand that we're not deserting her. She's going through something and I'm sure she didn't mean to take it out on you."

"Never mind that," Rayanne said with a wave of the hand. "I'm just wondering what we can do to help her, to let her know that we will always be there for each other."

Dorian returned to the den to join Rayanne and Ivory.

"I come bearing an olive branch," she said, looking ashamed. "Am I in the doghouse?"

"Of course you're not in the doghouse," Rayanne patted the seat beside her on the couch. "We all have our bad days. You're just having two in one," she said, and laughed, knowing the behavior Dorian was exhibiting was totally out of character for her.

"I was just being childish," Dorian said. "I'm sorry."

"This wouldn't have anything to do with my moving out next week?" Rayanne asked.

"No," Dorian lied and her eyes watered over slightly.

"Does it, Dorian?" Rayanne pressed. Dorian was her friend, more like a sister, and Rayanne wanted to help.

"It does seem that everyone I care about leaves me," Dorian said, and her eyes became sad.

"Dorian, I'll just be a phone call away," Rayanne said softly.

"I know, and I'm embarrassed about my behavior," Dorian said.

"No, you just found a way out of helping us do those damn dishes," Ivory joked.

"Dorian, always remember that it doesn't matter where we are in the world, we'll never really be apart because of how we feel about each other," Rayanne said. "You know I'll do anything for you."

"You can stay on here. Just kidding," Dorian teased. "I'm okay, really. "I'm just mourning the loss already."

"I'm not dead yet," Rayanne said, and laughed.

"I know, but I'm going to miss you like crazy," Dorian said.

"Dorian," Ivory began, "we love each other and nothing is ever gonna change that and although we may not always live under the same roof, we'll always be there for each other. You know us. We're the Manhattan Trio. We've got staying power," Ivory laughed and gave Dorian the high five. "That may not be a good choice of words, staying power, but you know what I mean."

Ivory and Dorian gave Rayanne a moving-out party and promised to spend many nights with her, and later that week they were with Rayanne when she moved into her new place.

The condo was done in luxurious fabrics, cool soft colors with huge windows that provided wonderful views of the city by day, but spectacular by night when the city was ablaze with a multitude of lights. The walls held trendy art pieces, and as a housewarming gift, Rayanne was given the piece they'd pooled their money and purchased at Patti's first art show. That was Rayanne's favorite piece of art and it was the one piece she dusted each week.

One evening shortly after the move, Rayanne was sitting on the side of her bed. She picked up the telephone and dialed Ralph's number.

"Hello?" he greeted her.

"Tell me, Mr. Underwood, are you in a wish-granting mood tonight?" she asked.

"That depends," he teased.

"Oh?"

"You know I'm just kidding. What's your wish?"

"Are you sure? Because it's going to take a lot of generosity to fulfill my wish."

"Just tell your fairy godfather and your wish is my command."

"I wish to spend the night in your arms."

"Your place or mine?"

"I'll be there in an hour."

Rayanne arrived at Ralph's apartment that evening wearing the full-length fur coat he had given her for Christmas a year ago, the same Christmas that Dorian received a diamond bracelet from Henry and Ivory, a Rolex watch from Eric.

Rayanne also wore a pair of black pumps and a

single red rose caught between her teeth. She let herself in with her key. Ralph was sitting on the couch with one leg propped up on the arm of the chair and one leg hanging in front of an open fire. He wore only a short silk robe.

She walked up to the back of the couch and kissed him on the neck.

"Hi," she said.

"You're late," he said, closing his eyes and inhaling her sweet, soft perfume.

"Is there anything I can do to make it up to you?"

"Oh, I don't know. I'll have to think about that," Ralph said, pretending to pout.

"Well," she said, coming around to the front of the couch and letting the coat slip to the floor, "I hope you don't take too long."

"Why? You going somewhere?"

"You tell me," she said, standing completely naked before him.

Ralph opened his eyes. "Baby," he said, catching his breath, and at the same time, a log fell in the fireplace, sending sparks up the chimney, but they were unmatched by the sparks Ralph felt inside. He reached out and touched her about the waist, allowing his hands to slide down to the curve of her hips. "You are beautiful."

"Am I forgiven?"

"Oh yes, yes." He pulled her to him and looked up into her eyes. "My God, woman, do you have any more ammunition in that arsenal of yours?"

"I won't tell. I like keeping little surprises for you."

He pulled her down onto the couch, loving her freshness, her energy, her spontaneity. They were so much a part of each other's lives and they shared so much now. Rayanne always felt that the substance of a good relationship was sharing everything, and that meant everything to her.

Ralph pulled Rayanne closer to him and kissed her passionately, and later as she nestled against him, she knew she couldn't be happier.

Early one morning, Rayanne opened the window to find a dark dull day in winter, the time of year when the clouds hung low in the heavens. On that cold day the wind hissed, tossing Rayanne's long, thick hair as she breathed in the crisp air. She pulled the burgundy terry cloth robe close to her body as she looked out over the city.

The parked vehicles were blanketed with a layer of snow, but because the streets in New York were always busy, the snow on the streets had already turned to slush. Rayanne loved the city. With all its pleasantries and its glory, she was fascinated by the bright lights and big-city atmosphere, the horse-drawn carriages and her many strolls along Central Park. She sighed and looked at Ralph, who was still asleep. She ran a comb through her hair and set the computer to print her latest project, and when the laser printer shot out the 108-page script, she turned off the machine and climbed back into bed.

"Where were you?" Ralph asked, sleep in his voice.

"I'm back now." She smoothed the covers up against her chin.

"You got a busy day planned?"

"It's too early to think right now. Ask me later." She nestled in her favorite place against him and they slept until noon.

* * *

Ralph arrived at Rayanne's three-bedroom condo at seven thirty that evening to escort her to the theater. It was the premier of her latest play, *The Ice Is Melting*. Although family and friends came from South Carolina to support Rayanne in her success, her parents had not made the trip but sent their love.

Ralph was handsome wearing his black tuxedo and Rayanne, the epitome of a young, rich, society woman, was radiant in a red floor-length dress and coat. The red shoes and purse and the diamond earrings that hung an inch below her earlobes completed her ensemble.

"You look fabulous," Ralph said, taking in her entire frame and kissing her on her cheek.

"You clean up pretty nicely yourself. What's this?" she asked, accepting the envelope that he handed her.

"The opera tickets."

"Thanks," she said, and put the tickets in the drawer of a table in the living room.

"Do we have time for a drink?" he asked.

"I don't think so." She looked at her watch. "We should be at the theater and in our seats at least by a quarter to seven."

Their limo stopped in front of the theater. Traffic moved up and down the streets, and the street was jammed with people entering the theater to see the play. Rayanne and Ralph met Ivory and Eric at the theater along with Dorian and a friend of hers whom they hadn't previously met. They were also joined by Greg and his wife, Cinnamon.

They sat through the three-act play and when

the curtains were drawn, they knew the play was a success. Rayanne had another hit on her hands.

Everything was going well until they caught sight of Henry and Olympia, and Rayanne knew how they happened to be there by the look Olympia gave Dorian when they were passing each other in the foyer.

Dorian, usually a chatterbox, was quiet.

"Are you all right?" Rayanne whispered to her. Dorian nodded her head that she was, but after the play and dinner at one of New York's finest restaurants, they went to Rayanne's condo for drinks.

Everyone noticed how Dorian completely ignored her date, but was hanging all over Ralph. Dorian kicked off her shoes, asked Ralph to dance. He obliged, she wrapped her arms around his neck, and they swayed, with closed eyes, to the music that someone was playing on the white baby grand piano located in a corner of the huge room. They whispered to each other and laughed out loud as though they shared a secret that the others weren't privy to. They danced to one song after the other and at times were so close to each other it became embarrassing for Rayanne and her guests.

During one of those dances when Ralph was holding Dorian a little too closely, he suddenly opened his eyes and noticed that they were the center of attention. He disengaged himself from Dorian, held her with one arm, and lifted the other in the air. "What's going on, guys?" he said in a slurred voice. "This is supposed to be a party."

"You two seem to be the only real party animals here," Ivory said curtly at the distasteful manner in which her friends were behaving.

Ralph looked from one face to the next. Then

his eyes came to settle on Rayanne's. He pulled away from Dorian's grip and made his way to a stool at the bar.

"Party poopers," Dorian giggled and sat in the chair next to her date.

Greg, a medium-height, stocky, middle-aged Caucasian man, and his wife got up and walked over to Rayanne. Kissing Rayanne on the cheek, he said, "Congratulations. Your play was a wonderful success. I'll call you tomorrow."

"Thanks for everything, Greg," she replied.

"Sure. Good night," he said.

"Congratulations again, Rayanne. Good night," Cinnamon said.

Rayanne walked them to the door.

Soon afterward, other guests left and as Ivory and Eric were about to leave, she approached Rayanne and said, "Congratulations, sweetheart, you've done it again. I'll call you tomorrow."

"Thanks, girlfriend," Rayanne said, and they embraced. "And thank you for coming, Eric."

"I enjoyed the play, and it was nice to see you all again," Eric said.

"Are you coming, Dorian?" Ivory called out.

"I may as well. It seems the party's over here," Dorian giggled.

They said good night. When Rayanne and Ralph were alone, he asked, "Why was everyone so mad?"

"You don't have any idea?" Rayanne asked. "You and Dorian behaved rather poorly, don't you think?"

"The girl was going through a hard time, seeing Henry and Olympia like that. I was just trying to help."

"Ralph, it's not your place to help Dorian out of

a spot like that. Dorian is where she is because she chooses to be there," Rayanne said. "You know I don't have a problem with you helping Dorian out of a tough situation, but the two of you were hanging all over each other like leeches."

"I'm sorry. I was just trying to help," Ralph said.

Rayanne left him there and she went into her bathroom and took a bubble bath. When she returned to the living room, Ralph was asleep on the couch. She covered him up and left him there to sleep. When she awoke the following morning, Ralph was gone.

Ralph accompanied Rayanne to the opera that evening. Upon entering the theater, they accepted programs and were ushered to their seats. There were a number of familiar faces and they smiled and bowed in recognition. Moments later, the lights dimmed, the curtains were drawn, and the program began. After several arias and at intermission, Ralph excused himself. Tiffany Berrington, a friend of Rayanne's, sat in his seat.

"Tiffany Berrington," Rayanne said. "I didn't know you were here."

Rayanne had met Tiffany at one of her plays and they had become friends. They were also on the board of directors of a major media corporation, and they'd even contemplated going into business together.

"I didn't know you were either until I saw Ralph a moment ago," Tiffany said.

"She's good, isn't she?" Rayanne said of the opera singer.

"Yes, she is," Tiffany said, and added, "We loved the play last week. Great opening night."

"Thank you. We thought it went well," Rayanne said, and after some discussion about the play, she asked, "Are Ted and Eliza here?"

Tiffany was married to Ted, and Eliza was their ten-year-old daughter.

"Ted is here. He's right over there," Tiffany said, pointing in his direction, and she and Rayanne waved to him. "But Eliza is at a sleepover at a friend's house. She's not much for the opera. She said the singers hurt her ears." She and Rayanne chuckled.

"She'll get into it a little later."

"I'm sure she will." Tiffany was wearing a blue gown that matched piercing blue eyes that sparkled with excitement as she asked, "Have you given any more thought to what we talked about? I know we can do this."

"Yes, and I should have an answer for you in a couple of weeks."

"This is a situation where we call all the shots and run it as we please. Each of us has contacts that will help greatly in getting this project off the ground and running in no time. We can't lose," Tiffany said enthusiastically, and Rayanne nodded in agreement. She knew that Tiffany was an excellent businesswoman and could hold her own in the boardroom with the power suits, but Rayanne also knew that it would be a lot of responsibility starting up a new business, and she wasn't sure how much time she'd be able to devote to the company. "We can do it," Tiffany said.

"You don't have to convince me. I just don't know whether we're going to have the kind of time it's going to take to get a new business started."

"We'll find the time. This will be our own personal baby. Think about it some more and we'll talk again."

"We'll talk soon."

"Great." Tiffany changed the subject. "Are you going to be available for that meeting in the morning?"

Tiffany's position as vice chairperson on the board allowed her the opportunity to assist in the decision-making process of the scripts selected for television movies.

"With the people from L.A.?" Rayanne asked. "I thought you were taking that meeting."

"I'd like you to be there with me on this one," Tiffany said.

"I'll be happy to accompany you, but I'm sure it won't be necessary. You are a much smarter negotiator than I."

"Two heads are better than one."

"Then, I'll be there," Rayanne said as the lights began to dim.

"Great. Well, I suppose I'd better get back into my seat."

"Say hello to Ted and Eliza."

"I will," Tiffany said, and winked at Rayanne. "See you in the morning."

Tiffany left just as Ralph rejoined Rayanne.

"Hey you," Rayanne said as Ralph slid back into his seat beside her.

"Hey yourself," he said.

When the singer concluded her final number and curtsied, she received a standing ovation and "encore" could be heard across the house. The singer did one last song and the program came to an end. The theater emptied out onto the street, and people went in different directions.

"Would you like to stop off for a drink?" Ralph asked.

"Not tonight. I've got a meeting in the morning and I need to prepare," Rayanne said.

Rayanne and Ralph hadn't spoken all week. She had been busy with projects, but he was thinking that she was still angry at him. He wanted to be close to her again, but he also knew not to rock the boat and to give her the time she needed. She'd come around soon, Ralph thought, or he hoped.

"Are you sure you don't want to have just one drink?" he asked.

"No, really, I can't. I've got a couple of things that I need to review tonight."

"This is against my better judgment, but if this is what you want," he joked.

Rayanne knew Ralph didn't like her being angry at him. She opened her eyes, looked at him, and said, "What if I cooked you dinner tomorrow night?" She smiled and placed a finger on the tip of his nose. "Would that make up for tonight?"

"Just so you know, I'm not happy about this," he said, and laughed.

"I'll make it up to you. Deal?" she asked.

He looked at her and said, "Deal," and he kissed her on the lips, happy now that she no longer appeared to be angry at him.

Chapter 13

Rayanne had been home no more than a half hour from a late afternoon tea party that was held at a friend's home, when Ralph arrived that evening. She greeted him at the door wearing, over her red silk panties and camisole, a matching see-through negligee that swept the floor as she walked. She also wore red fishnet hose and red spiked heels. A classical piece played on the CD player in the background.

"Oh, it's you," she said, pretending she was expecting someone else. She closed the door and walked into the den with Ralph following.

"Who did you expect?" he asked, thinking how great she looked.

"I thought you were the other guy," she teased.

"Oh, I must be at the wrong place. The girl I came to see tonight is the girl I planned to take on a little trip to Bermuda." He flashed the tickets.

Rayanne turned to him, spun him around, and pushed him toward the front door.

"Let's start this evening all over," she said, opening the door. "Now, you go back out and ring the doorbell again. I'll answer, you show me the tickets. I'll be totally surprised and we'll go from there." She pushed him out the door and closed it behind him. The doorbell was silent. *What's taking him so long? I'll give him another thirty seconds.* Silence. She opened the door to find Ralph walking away.

"Ralph," she called after him. "Where are you going?" He looked back, smiled but continued to walk away.

Where is he going? Rayanne thought as she dashed inside, grabbed a robe, and slipped into it. She rushed back to the door. She remembered once before when Ralph was in one of his moods and she had toyed with him this way. He'd left and she didn't see or hear from him for three days. *I'd better catch up with him,* she thought, but as she flung open the door, Ralph was standing there smiling.

"Gotcha," he said, pointing a finger at her, and glided into her condo.

"Why, you . . . you," she said.

"Now do you want to start this evening over?" he asked, a crooked smile on his face.

She nodded yes.

"Teach you to play games with me," he laughed.

"You won this time," she said, and kissed him on his cheek.

"Now, that's more like it," he said, rubbing his hands together in front of the open fire. "It is cold out there tonight."

"A cup of coffee will knock that chill right off." She was about to go off to the kitchen.

"Not just yet," he said, pulling her to him. "Sit with me for a while." He removed his top coat, threw it across a chair, and they sat on the couch together.

"How was your day?" he asked.

"I had several meetings today," she replied. "What about you?"

"It was busy."

Rayanne kissed Ralph lightly on the lips and they sat quietly and watched the fire flicker while Tchaikovsky's "Swan Lake" played softly in the background.

"I cooked dinner here for you tonight," Rayanne said.

Rayanne had learned to cook long ago and she enjoyed cooking for Ralph and she would surprise him on occasions with one of his favorite meals.

"Something smells good," he said.

"I'm working on another play," Rayanne said. "I hope Greg will be successful in selling this one."

"What do you call this masterpiece?"

"I wouldn't call it that. You do remember how many I've written that were rejected. Anyway this one is called *Out of the Darkness*," she answered.

"That sounds ominous."

"Yes, but quite the contrary. I'll tell you about it in a minute, but first, come with me. I want you to have a little taste. Just enough to whet your appetite," she said, running a finger down the side of his face.

Ralph obeyed, following her into the kitchen. Rayanne had made beef Wellington and all the things that he liked to go with it, and although Ralph loved her cooking, there was something else he wanted to talk with her about.

"You said you wanted to talk with me about something?" Rayanne asked, looking back over her shoulder at Ralph.

"I want to talk about us," he said.

"What about us? Is something wrong?"

"I think we should get married."

"You do?" Rayanne said.

Ralph had been dropping hints for some time, and whenever he did, she told him she'd think about it.

Ralph said, "Yes, I do."

"Okay, I'll think about it."

"You've been thinking about it for the past year now," he reminded her.

"Here, taste this," she said, after cutting off an edge of the meat and cooling it with her breath before sticking it into his mouth.

"Rayanne, I'm serious about this," he said, chewing and swallowing the meat. "I don't want to live alone anymore."

"I know." She paused a moment trying to find the right words. She'd given him an acceptable answer each time he'd approached the subject of marriage, but tonight she couldn't find the right words. Instead she said, "What do you think?" Seeing the puzzled look on his face, she said, "About the meat?"

"Delicious, but when are you going to give me an answer to my proposal?"

"Soon, my darling. I promise you. Soon. Now, come back with me and relax. Dinner will be ready shortly." She poured each of them a glass of wine, and they sat on the couch. Rayanne fluffed some pillows, put them under his head, and undid his tie.

She kneeled on the floor beside the couch, untied his shoes, and lifted his feet up onto the sofa. She massaged his feet and told him about the play.

When she finished, he said, "I don't know how you do it."

"I suppose you could call it using my imagination," Rayanne laughed. "I just write about things that are happening in the world today and just flavor them with my own imagination, characters, a little humor, compassion, sensitivity, and sometimes it works."

"Even for the misses, you've still got a hell of a track record. Beauty and brains."

Rayanne changed the subject. "Tiffany and I are considering starting up a typing service together. The great thing about this is that we already have start-up capital. We have enough seed money to get the building, equipment, everything," Rayanne said excitedly. "Tiffany and I have been running the idea around in our heads. Tell me what you think."

"It sounds like a great idea, but with your schedule, will you have the time to commit to the day-to-day operation of a new business? You know starting a business from the ground up, it would have to be a hands-on situation until it is up and running," he said.

"We would have to make time," Rayanne said, but that had been her thinking exactly. "Getting people properly trained and all, but we can do it."

It was as though she was trying to convince herself more than Ralph.

After dinner, they returned to the den with their coffee. Ralph didn't touch his coffee until it was just barely warm, and Rayanne wondered why he just didn't ask for iced coffee since he always seemed to like it best when it was cold.

"I just don't want to see you overextend yourself and get all stressed out," Ralph said soothingly.

"I certainly won't extend so much that we won't have time for each other," she assured him. "We've given some serious thought to this and I think I want to do it." Rayanne found the more she talked about the typing service, the more she was convinced she wanted to do it.

"Then what can I say? Go for it," he said.

Rayanne loved this man's supportiveness of her and her career choices. Recently, she'd been recognized as a young, savvy businesswoman, and Ralph wasn't threatened by her independence, nor was he intimidated by her aggressiveness or accomplishments. If anything, her talents endeared her to him. He was wonderful, he was thoughtful, and he should be rewarded, she thought. She'd pamper him, spoil him, and make all his fantasies come true, she thought as she turned her full attention to him.

Ralph and Rayanne spent the next week in Bermuda. She'd never been there before, but everything Ralph had told her about the island was true as well. Ralph received a call from his office before the week was up, and he cut his trip short, but Ivory and Dorian were able to join Rayanne, and they spent a couple of days enjoying the island.

That following winter, *Out of the Darkness* opened on Broadway and became Rayanne's biggest hit of all. The play evoked so much emotion that there was hardly a dry eye in the audience.

Chapter 14

Dorian and Ivory arrived at Rayanne's condo a little after ten that Saturday morning. "What are you two doing here at this hour?" Rayanne said, allowing them to enter, and they headed back to her bedroom. "I could've had an attitude, you know," Rayanne joked.

"You never have an attitude, but anyway, what are your plans for today?" Dorian asked. Picking up a magazine from the magazine rack in the bedroom, she sat on the bed and flipped through the pages.

"I was just finishing up some contracts for the office," Rayanne explained.

"How is business at Raytiff?" Ivory asked.

Rayanne and Tiffany had combined their names and came up with Raytiff as the name for their typing service. Their business had opened for service six months ago and it was going very well, and Rayanne thanked the girls for sending business to them.

"We have gotten a lot of customers that you guys referred to us and we thank you," Rayanne said.

"Of course," Ivory said.

"I got a thank-you card from Tiffany," Dorian said.

"So did I," Ivory commented.

"So, what's up?" Rayanne asked. "How are you guys doing?"

"We thought we'd go by the club and play a little tennis, do a little shopping, and have something to eat," Dorian said, getting bored with the magazine. She returned it to the rack and began looking through Rayanne's closet. She selected a blouse, a belt, and a scarf and tossed them onto the bed. The girls still searched through each other's closets and borrowed from each other. It was an old habit that they never broke. Ivory and Rayanne sat on the bed. Dorian walked over to the dresser and checked her makeup, eyeing her face closely, gently touching the areas under her eyes and the corners of her mouth.

"What are you looking at, Dorian?" Rayanne asked. She was paying more attention to her face than usual.

"Wrinkles," Dorian replied.

"Girl, please," Rayanne said.

"I have told her a million times that wrinkles are a long way away, but if she keeps worrying about them, she's gonna wake up one morning looking like somebody's grandma," Ivory said, and they laughed. "Worrying is a sure way to get them."

"That's for sure," Rayanne agreed, but she had noticed dark circles around Dorian's eyes on occasion.

Dorian pinched her cheeks, which immediately colored into a healthy pink. She turned away from the mirror. "I'm trying not to use as much makeup."

"You really don't need to wear any makeup at all. Your complexion is beautiful," Rayanne said.

"Do you really think so?" Dorian asked, a little skeptically.

"Absolutely," Rayanne said, and she changed the subject. "Hey, I bought a new racket yesterday."

"You did. I need a new one, myself," Dorian said, and turned back to the mirror to apply a little mascara.

"Sure. You need a new tennis racket like you need a hole in your head," Rayanne said. Then she looked at Ivory. "You're quiet today, sweetie. What's going on with you?"

"I met a man," Ivory said, getting up and walking over to the magazine rack. But that wasn't new. Ivory was always meeting a man, only she hadn't dated anyone on a steady basis, except Eric, since Cal's death. "This is the real thing this time."

"Yeah, this is the real deal," Dorian agreed, wetting her finger with her tongue and running it over an eyebrow. "She's gone, hook, line, and sinker."

"What's so special about this one?" Rayanne asked.

"She's in love with this one," Dorian said, and looked at them and then back in the mirror.

"Dorian, please shut up," Rayanne said, and threw a pillow at her.

"But it's true," Dorian said, picked up the pillow, and threw it on the bed.

Rayanne got up and sat behind Ivory, where she sat on the foot of the bed, and Rayanne wrapped both arms around her. "So, what's wrong with my girl?" she asked. She'd never seen Ivory like that before.

Ivory was a person who constantly celebrated life. Nothing was unobtainable to her. She could bring excitement to trivial things, she was delightful and energetic, and above all, Ivory had an undying love for people.

"What's going on with you?" Rayanne wanted to know.

"Oh, nothing," Ivory said with a wave of her hand.

But Rayanne knew that wasn't true. She remembered once when they were in elementary school and one of their classmates, who was less fortunate, didn't have money for lunch, Ivory gave that classmate her own lunch money. There were times when she missed the bus and walked to school because of doing something to help an elderly person or someone else who needed help. That was Ivory, the happy-go-lucky, fun-loving girl. But she was different now, and Rayanne was concerned. She didn't want her to return to the depressed state she'd experienced after Cal's death.

"Come on, this is me. Out with it. I have never seen you like this. I don't see you guys for a couple of weeks and you go crazy on me. Come on, spit it out," Rayanne coaxed, rocking back and forth with her arms still tied around Ivory.

"Rayanne, I met this man," Ivory said.

"Okay. I think I understand that much. Is he making you unhappy?"

"No. Absolutely not," Ivory answered, shaking her head vigorously.

"He makes you happy, then?"

"Yes, very happy." She nodded.

"Then I don't understand," Rayanne said, removing her arms.

"I met Desmond two months ago and we liked each other right away, but I was involved with Eric, and you know Eric. He's been so good to me. He helped me put it back together all those years ago, so I didn't want to hurt him." Eric was patient and understanding of Ivory when she was going through some rough patches, and she appreciated him very much.

"I can understand your loyalty to Eric, but obviously you must feel something special for this Desmond, who I'm just hearing about for the first time," Rayanne said.

"I fell in love with Desmond," Ivory said.

"So, what's wrong with that? He's not married, is he?" Rayanne asked. Ivory shook her head. "You said you love him, he makes you happy, and he's not married. So what's the problem? Do you love Eric also?"

"I'm not in love with Eric, if that's what you mean, but he's a great guy, and he doesn't want to let me go," Ivory said.

"I'm sure he doesn't, but it really isn't his call, is it?" Rayanne said. When Ivory said she felt she owed Eric more than that, Rayanne said, "You guys dated, you had some good times, but it's over. You're moving on."

"When I met Desmond, there was just so much chemistry between us. I've never felt this way about anyone. I want to spend the rest of my life with him and I told him so," Ivory said.

"Okay," Rayanne pressed.

"Eric and I were together two weeks ago, and I told him I thought we should start seeing other people. Well, he hit the ceiling, said he wasn't interested in seeing other people, and he doesn't want me to see anyone else either."

"You didn't agree to that, did you?" Rayanne asked.

"Well, sort of."

"Ivory," Rayanne said, not totally surprised, knowing Ivory's devious nature.

"It's all very confusing. Anyway, I have a strong attraction for Eric. We are compatible in many ways and I thought maybe I was making a mistake limiting my dating to just one man." Ivory seemed confused, but she tried to explain, "There was a time when I thought of ending my relationship with Desmond because I felt I owed Eric, but I couldn't stop seeing him, Desmond, I mean. We have a lot in common too, we talk about everything, he's wonderful," she said.

Rayanne was more confused now than ever. "Ivory, you said you're in love with Desmond, he was the apple of your eye. You care about Eric, but you are not in love with him. Then, what's the problem? Desmond sounds like a man who's after my own heart."

"Eric has been great. He's in love with me."

"I understand that, Ivory, but you have to make a decision."

"I know," Ivory said thoughtfully.

"You love Desmond. Eric will just have to take a hike."

"It's the age thing," Dorian said, when Ivory didn't respond.

"What age thing?" Rayanne asked, and laughed. "Oh, is he one of those older gentlemen?"

"That might've been better. Rayanne, I'm twenty-six," Ivory said. Rayanne raised her eyebrows, waiting for Ivory to continue. "Desmond's only twenty and I'm in love with him. The last few weeks, he's made me happier than I've ever been."

"Ivory, you love the man. He makes you happy. What am I missing? I really don't see what the issue is. I think you should go with it," Rayanne said, lifting her hands in the air.

"Be honest with me, Ray. What would you do if you were in my shoes?" Ivory asked.

"Ivory, I am in your shoes. Well, vice versa," Rayanne said.

"That's different. Society is always more accepting of an older man and a younger woman than the other way around. What will people think?"

Rayanne asked, "Since when have you cared about what people think?"

"I suppose since I met Desmond."

"Ivory, you have to live for yourself. Your happiness is what's important. This is life, and life is for living, giving, and experiencing everything. Passion, pain, happiness, sadness, successes, disappointments, all of it. This is no dress rehearsal, Ivory," Rayanne said. "This is what's happening now."

"God, when I'm fifty, he'll only be forty-two."

"Yeah, and when you're sixty, he'll be fifty-two. What's the difference? Someone said to me once, do the things today that make you happy because a hundred years from now, we'll all be dead and it won't matter. Be happy, girl. Look at us. We've got it all. We are right where we want to be."

"I am happy," Ivory said halfheartedly.

"Then, don't go bringing in obstacles where there are none. Take today for what it's worth and go with it. That's my motto." With that Rayanne gave a little laugh. Her friend had really fallen in love.

"Yeah." Ivory got up from the bed and headed toward the kitchen. She turned at the door and said, "I like that. A hundred years from now, we'll all be dead and it won't matter." Ivory laughed that infectious laugh as her beautiful face lit up. "So, are you gonna get dressed or lie around here all day?" she said, going toward the refrigerator. Rayanne laughed and shook her head.

"I'll say the chick is feeling better. She's hungry,"

Dorian said, finishing her makeup. She removed the beret from her hair and the blond hair fell, cascading down her back.

"That girl wants to be black so bad," Ivory called out over her shoulder.

"Where in the world did she meet someone with the name Desmond?" Rayanne whispered to Dorian, and they laughed.

"I heard that and it's none of your damn business," Ivory snapped in good humor.

"Yeah, the girl is back," Rayanne said.

After playing a couple of sets of tennis, they sat in the steam room an hour. Each had facials, their nails manicured, and then they ate lunch. Afterward, they went to Tiffany's, where Ivory ordered a set of china, Dorian bought a pair of diamond earrings, which she vowed she'd have Henry reimburse her for later, and Rayanne purchased three business suits, one navy, one beige, and one black, and blouses to match each suit. She also purchased a baby-blue chiffon dress, which she intended to wear to the opera in two weeks to see *Madame Butterfly*. This dress she'd keep, unlike times in the past when they wanted something for a special function, and, at Ivory's prompting, went into an expensive shop, charged something fancy only to wear it, have it cleaned, if necessary, and return it after the function. But now they'd arrived. They could afford any dress in the store. They could wear it once and hang it in the closet for all eternity, if they chose. They no longer had to resort to that kind of tactic.

When they arrived at Bloomingdale's, Ivory attacked the racks and within minutes she held a half dozen items over her arm, which she began to trying on. She was a girl on a mission, as Rayanne and Dorian watched with raised eyebrows. They got a kick out of shopping with Ivory. It was an adventure watching her switch jackets and skirts with others that didn't match and come out of the dressing room, shocking the girls, making them hysterical with laughter. Some of the outfits made Ivory look like someone who'd wandered onto Earth from some other planet. Before the girls ended their day of pampering and buying things for themselves, each girl bought a special gift for the others, which is something they did often.

Chapter 15

What a day, Rayanne thought. It was rainy and very cold. The weather was behaving like a spoiled child and it was making everyone miserable. She wasn't just pissed off with the weather. There was another reason for the bad mood she found herself in when she awoke before daybreak. She received a call from home telling her that her brother, Josh, had been arrested for disorderly conduct. He'd been drinking, gotten into a fight, and been arrested. By the time she received the call, Josh was out of jail, but the situation had put her parents under a lot of stress. *Why did Josh keep doing things like that?* she wondered.

She and Tiffany had rented a suite of offices on the Upper East Side and had hired an office manager and four typists. It was a busy and hectic time and when things finally slowed down, summer, her favorite time of year for traveling, was over and she had missed it. Nevertheless, she decided she was going to treat herself to some real fun anyway. It was time. She decided to go out and party and let her hair down for a change. And she did, and only after she had partied until she was completely worn out did she decide to get a taxi home.

She left the club, walked out onto the street, and before she could get a taxi, some stranger walked up to her and demanded she give him her purse. Well, she thought that purse belonged to her and she had no intention of turning it over to him. He had other plans, however, and when she put up resistance, he struck her in the face and threw her to the ground.

The police were called and she filed a report, but she knew nothing would come of it. Dozens of people were mugged or killed daily in the city, and she was just another statistic. She was so sick of the violence.

As she drank coffee and chewed up two aspirins, she thought that mugger had better be glad that she was tired and almost drunk; otherwise she would've creamed him. And that was true. Rayanne had grown up with brothers who really knew how to defend themselves, and they'd taught Rayanne as well. But she had been caught by surprise and was totally defenseless, and she had lost. She was so upset when she went to bed that she had trouble falling asleep. With all that was happening in her life lately, it was no wonder that when she woke, she had a bad headache and was in a foul frame of mind. She sat on the couch, put her feet up, and waited for the pills to work.

She tried to form in her mind what needed to be done that day, but exhaustion took over and she dozed off. When she awoke later, the day had dawned clearer and sunnier than it had been in weeks.

Rayanne got up and touched a button, and as the drapes opened the length of the wall, the room was flooded with light. She gave the sky a measuring glance, then sat at her desk and made notes on things she needed to do at the office and at home. She had become so busy that she'd become a list person, and without lists she'd be lost. There was something else that was occupying her mind lately. She wanted to go back to school. Ivory and Dorian had gotten their master's, but she hadn't found the time to go back herself. *Soon,* she thought.

When her lists were completed, she dressed in a pair of white wool slacks, a white silk blouse, and a coral wool jacket. She slipped her feet into a pair of white ankle boots, picked up her purse from the bed, and headed out. She stepped out of a taxi in front of Elayne's Salon, where she went every Saturday to have her hair and nails done. She sat in the chair and a cup of black coffee was placed on the table in front of her. She took a sip and settled back and allowed Elayne to take care of her. As she closed her eyes, she thought of the list she'd made and which she left on her bed. She tried to reconstruct the list in her mind. The only things she could remember were the drapes and comforter she wanted to order.

Although the afternoon sun was amazingly clear for that time of year and the sun was so bright it hurt her eyes, Rayanne could see the clouds rolling across the edge of the sky, gathering in the east, and she wondered whether it would snow again soon and cover the city in a soft blanket of whiteness. She spent much of that day on the telephone, but that was the way it had been. She'd been moving nonstop the past few months and as she was contemplating where she'd spend the holidays, the telephone rang. It was Ivory. A new club had just opened and she thought they should check it out. They'd meet first for dinner, then on to the club for dancing.

Rayanne went into the bathroom and stared at the bruise on her cheek. Yes, she'd been the victim of yet another mugging and nothing was new. The mugger wanted her purse and she put up resistance and, pow, she got it again. Right in the face. Couldn't they hit her some place other than her face? As she looked at her face she thought a little makeup would probably cover up the bruise so that it wouldn't be too noticeable.

She gently washed her face, patted it dry, and applied a light layer of pink facial mask. Afterward, she laid out a short straight black skirt and a black and white blouse. Then she rinsed the mask from her face. She put on a moisturizer, poured herself a cup of coffee, and lay back on the couch to read the newspaper. Crime was on the rise: three robberies, two stabbings, and two shootings.

At dinner, although Dorian was having one of her favorite meals, she hardly touched the food, other than move it from one place to another on her plate. *And wasn't she getting thinner?* Rayanne thought. She looked up to see Ivory staring at her.

"What happened to your face?" Ivory asked.

"Oh, it's nothing." Rayanne tried to brush it off with a wave of the hand.

Ivory said, looking closer, "Your face is bruised and it looks swollen."

Rayanne sat quietly for a moment. "I was mugged again last night," she confessed.

"What?" Ivory said, her face clouded with concern.

"Yeah. Some guy wanted my purse again and

as usual, I refused and, pow," she said. "You know the routine."

"Rayanne, I keep telling you. It's just not smart to try to fight off a mugger. Give them what they want, no matter what it is. It's not worth your life or having them use you as a punching bag. These people are crazy out of their heads, all drugged out," Ivory said. "You know what they say about living in New York. Keep mugger's money on you at all times. It sometimes saves your life. Are you okay?"

"Other than being thoroughly pissed, I'm fine. Sometimes I think I walk down the street with a huge stamp on my forehead that reads, *hey, mug me. I'm an easy target.*"

"It's nothing to joke about," Dorian said.

"That's right," Ivory agreed.

"I know," Rayanne said.

After dinner, they left the restaurant and went to the club. The music was jumping, the club was filled to its capacity, and the dance floor was crowded. After a while, the girls found three available seats at the bar.

"This place is slamming," Ivory said.

"I love that song," Dorian said. She got up from the stool and danced her way to the floor with Ivory and Rayanne behind her. They danced together until three men joined them on the dance floor. They danced until two in the morning.

In the taxi home, Dorian took a small container from her purse and snorted the white substance from it. "Dorian, what are you doing?" Rayanne's whisper came out in a hiss.

"I've told her about this shit," Ivory said, then looked at Dorian. "We offered to help you, but you say you don't have a problem. You don't think cocaine is a problem? Dorian, that shit kills."

"Dorian, you have got to stop this," Rayanne warned.

"Why do you guys think I've got a problem?"

"Because you damn well do," Ivory said through clenched teeth. "I don't want you to die and I'll be damned if I'll watch you kill yourself."

"I'm not going to kill myself," Dorian said.

"Oh no," Ivory spat out.

"Dorian, we just want to help you," Rayanne said more gently this time.

"If you girls don't blow my high tonight, I promise I'll talk about my so-called problem tomorrow," Dorian said.

The taxi pulled up in front of the loft, but they didn't want Dorian spending the night alone, since Ivory had moved in with Desmond. Rayanne gave instructions to the driver to take them to her condo, where Dorian spent the night. Before Ivory left, they helped Dorian get settled in Rayanne's spare bedroom.

Night was just beginning to fall when Rayanne dashed out of the office, took a taxi, and met Dorian and Ivory at a Midtown restaurant. She hadn't seen the girls in a while and she'd missed them. They had dinner and did some catching up.

"So, how are both of you?" Rayanne asked.

"Great," Ivory said. "What about you?"

"Busy as usual."

"You're always busy," Ivory said. "You should give yourself a break. Take it easy."

"There's still so much that I want to do," Rayanne replied.

Dorian said, "How are the folks?"

"Fine. I talked with them earlier and they sent you their love," Rayanne said. "How is it going with you, Dorian?"

"I'm fine," she replied.

"Are you still seeing that guy who you said hit you?" Rayanne asked.

"Who?" Dorian asked.

"I don't know who the psycho is," Rayanne said. "I would no more see a man who beats me than I would a rattlesnake."

"She likes a man who tries to tear her eyes out," Ivory said. "I would've kicked his ass to the curb long ago."

"What's going on with Henry? You're gonna be his mistress for the rest of your life?" Ivory said.

"Dorian, that ship has sailed. You don't need this," Rayanne said.

"That's right. He's been blowing smoke for ten years. Hell, I'd get rid of him and that psycho and get on with my life," Ivory said. "Make up your mind what you're gonna do with your life."

"If I remember correctly, it wasn't long ago when you were in the same situation, or at least you couldn't decide what you wanted," Dorian said.

"That situation was completely different," Ivory said.

"Ivory, give me a break, will you?" Dorian said. "I want you to answer one question for me."

"What's that?" Ivory asked.

"Where are we spending Thanksgiving this year and who's bringing the doggone turkey?"

Chapter 16

The phone rang at a quarter to nine. Rayanne almost never opened an eye on a Saturday morning before ten thirty. She thought about letting the machine pick it up, but she answered it instead. It was Ivory. She was scheduled to go to California on assignment and wanted to let Rayanne know.

"When are you leaving?" Rayanne asked.

"I've got an eleven o'clock flight out today," Ivory replied.

"Today?"

"Yes. In just a couple of hours. They want to do a shoot in Los Angeles, would you believe, tomorrow of all days? Can you imagine that? And from there we go to San Francisco. I should be back by Tuesday. Wednesday, the latest."

"Well, have a good trip," Rayanne said. "You talked with Dorian lately?"

That was another reason for Ivory's call.

"You'll need to keep an eye on her while I'm away. Desmond will as well."

"Of course I will," Rayanne said, her head still in a buzz from lack of sleep. The typing service was getting so much work that Rayanne and Tiffany hired four additional typists and Rayanne was working on another play. "Ivory, when you get back, I think we need to have another talk with Dorian. I'm worried about her."

"It's been bothering me too," Ivory shared.

Both Rayanne and Ivory noticed that Dorian had started using an assortment of drugs. She'd even smoked crack in their presence a couple of times. They'd talked with Dorian, reminding her of the dangers of abusing drugs, with Dorian always promising that she'd cut back, but never a promise to quit.

"Dorian got beat up again last night."

"What happened?" Rayanne asked, sitting up in bed. "Is she all right?"

"Someone she met at a bar whacked her around last night. I don't know, Rayanne, Dorian is flirting with anyone who wears pants and I keep telling her that if she isn't careful, something like this could happen to her."

Rayanne turned in bed, putting her feet on the floor. Ralph stirred in bed beside her, but he didn't wake up. "Has she seen a doctor or called the police?"

"She doesn't even know who hit her and her face is black and blue, but she says it's not as bad as it looks."

Rayanne sprang out of bed and was on her feet. "I'm coming over," she said.

"There is no need. She's got a steak on it and it's looking better. Besides, she is meeting Henry for lunch in a couple of hours."

"How is she going to explain those bruises to Henry?"

"She's gonna tell him she was mugged."

"Lord," was all Rayanne could say.

Ivory looked at her watch. "Rayanne, I've gotta get out of here or I'll miss my flight."

"Okay. Have a good trip and don't worry about Dorian. We'll check in on her."

"Okay, and I'll see you when I get back," Ivory said, and handed Dorian the phone. After talking with Dorian and being assured that she was fine and would call her when she returned from lunch, Rayanne hung up and sat down on the side of the bed. She was in deep concentration when she felt the pressure of Ralph's hand pulling her to him.

"Get back into bed," he said. Rayanne obeyed. She was silent as she lay in bed. "Who were you talking with so early in the morning?" he asked, snuggling close to her. Rayanne relayed her conversation with Ivory to him. "What are you talking about?" Ralph asked, finally opening his eyes and looking bewildered.

"Dorian was beaten up by some guy she met at a bar last night and she is black and blue," Rayanne said.

Ralph let out a little whistle. "Is she all right?"

"She said she is, but I still don't like it. He had no right hitting her."

"Honey, Dorian's a big girl. She can take care of herself," Ralph said.

"That's not the point, and obviously, not true," Rayanne said. "If it were, Dorian wouldn't be at home black and blue with a piece of steak on her face right now."

Ralph propped himself up on an elbow and stared dismally at Rayanne. "What do you want to do?" he asked.

"There's nothing to do. She's meeting Henry in a couple of hours."

"That should be interesting," Ralph said.

"Dorian shouldn't be putting that stuff in her body either."

"Why don't you call it what it is? It's cocaine. It's not a dirty word. You don't have to treat it that way," Ralph said, and the smile lines in his face seemed more pronounced.

"I know what it is, Ralph, and I wish I didn't have to deal with it at all, but it's there staring me in the face and it concerns me, okay?"

"Why are we talking about this now?"

"Honey, drugs kill and I have a desire for us all to grow old together."

"Rayanne, I know what you are getting at and I'm not an addict, I'm not hooked on the stuff. I just do it sometimes. I can quit any time I want."

"I sure wish you would want to."

"I can't see what the big deal is."

"Ralph, drugs are a big part of the problems we're having in this country today, and if we don't take some responsibility for ourselves and educate others, then we are doomed. I need you to promise me that you will do something about the drugs."

"You're serious, aren't you?"

"Yes, I am."

"Okay, baby. I love you and I don't want to lose you, so if you want me to quit, I will. You are too important to me for me to let something like this come between us."

"You promise?"

"I promise," Ralph said. Then he said, "Now can we go back to sleep?"

As Rayanne lay there thinking about the situation,

she knew she couldn't stand by and do nothing, but how could she help when she wasn't sure that her friends wanted the help she was offering? Suddenly, she heard Ralph snoring, nestled there beside her. She looked at the clock and although it was still early, Rayanne couldn't get back to sleep.

Chapter 17

The hour was late but the cocktail party was in full swing. It was Labor Day weekend and Rayanne and Ivory were throwing a party before Rayanne returned to school. Rayanne was planning to take a course in public speaking. Dorian had flown to Paris three days earlier to spend two glorious weeks, which she referred to as a minivacation, with Henry, who was still married but insisted he was getting a divorce without involving Dorian more than was necessary, and he was being as discreet and protective of her as he could be. He just hadn't gotten the divorce as he'd promised and he hadn't married Dorian.

The food was catered to the condo, the guests milled around, getting acquainted, dancing, and listening to wonderful numbers being played by an elegantly dressed woman who sat at the piano, while bursts of laughter punctuated the conversation. A combination of cigarette and marijuana smoke mingled and drifted across the room. Some of the guests munched on food, some did lines of cocaine, while others gorged themselves on liquor or wine or whatever was available at that hour. Rayanne and Ralph danced closely, their bodies molded, and kept perfect pace as he kissed her on her lips. When the kiss ended, Rayanne smiled and Ralph whispered in her ear, "You're so beautiful."

Rayanne had lightened her hair to a reddish brown, and she wore it high on top of her head, with wisps about her neck. Her dark brown eyes sparkled with happiness and excitement. She wore black spiked heels, black silk nylons, a black sheer sleeveless top, and a floor-length black skirt, slit high up her thigh. "I love you, honey," he said, holding her close. She closed her eyes, enjoying the dance. Ivory and Desmond were dancing and chatting and Rayanne was thrilled to see how happy they were.

When the phone rang, Ivory answered it. She was dressed in a white floor-length dress that covered her throat up front but plunged dangerously close to her behind in back, and she wore white pumps and white accessories. The one thing that was in keeping with her name was that Ivory almost always wore white. It was her favorite color, if you could call white a color.

Ivory beckoned a smiling Rayanne to the phone. Rayanne's smile vanished when she saw the expression on Ivory's face.

"What is it?" Rayanne asked.

Ivory handed her the phone. "It's your mom." Ivory put her hands to her mouth and moved to Rayanne's side.

"Mama, what's going on?" Rayanne asked, knowing whatever it was, it was serious for her mother to call at that hour.

"It's your daddy, honey. He's in the hospital."

"What's wrong with Daddy?" she asked, walking into another room, away from the noise and the crowd. Ralph walked over to Rayanne. "How is he, Mama? And what about you?"

"Don't you worry about me, I'm fine. We just have to be strong for your daddy and trust in the Lord," Helen said.

"I'll be there as quickly as I can," Rayanne said. When the conversation ended, she relayed the news to Ralph and Ivory as tears rolled down her face.

"Mama said the doctors are optimistic, but he's not out of the woods yet," Rayanne said.

"I'm sorry, baby," Ralph said, taking her into his arms. "Is there anything I can do?"

"I've got to get home," Rayanne said, wiping away her tears.

"When do we leave?" Ivory asked.

Rayanne called Lila. She got the answering machine. "Lila, this is Rayanne. If you're there, please pick up." No one answered. "Lila, please pick up the phone," Rayanne said, fighting back the tears that threatened to flow again.

Ivory snatched the phone from Rayanne's hand. "Lila, pick up the goddamn phone. This is no time to be pussyfooting around. Pick up the goddamn phone." Lila had never liked receiving late night or early morning phone calls. Her philosophy was that such calls always brought bad news, and that whatever it was that had happened she couldn't do anything about it. It would be wise to get a good night's sleep to be able to handle the situation when she did receive the news. Rayanne left a short message on the machine informing Lila that she would be taking the first available flight back home, since all she could get on that holiday weekend when Ivory called the airport was a standby flight.

At nine o'clock the following morning, Rayanne boarded a plane and was on her way to South Carolina. Upon arriving at the airport, she rented a car and drove directly to the hospital.

The hospital was a little different than she remembered when she had her tonsils removed when she was eight years old. Eighteen years was a long time and things change. Even the nurses no longer wore the crisp and businesslike white uniforms. Their uniforms now were pastel colors, but they still carried themselves with that air of professionalism that went along with the pride they felt for their contribution to the medical profession.

Rayanne entered the waiting room on the fourth floor, her eyes scanning the room until they met those of her mother's. Rayanne was the youngest of three brothers and two sisters, and everyone was there except Lila, whom she had tried to reach the night before.

Lila was divorced four years ago, and she lived in New York with her thirteen-year-old son, Jeremy. Rayanne didn't know how Perry had managed to stay married to Lila for as long as he had because she was a royal bitch. I guess love does make you do crazy things and, he did.

Rayanne rushed over and embraced her mother. "How are you, Mama?"

"I'm fine, baby. How's my girl?" her mother replied.

"I'm okay. What about Daddy? What are the doctors saying now?"

"Take that buckle out of your brow." Her mother smiled and lifted a hand to touch her daughter's cheek. "Your daddy gave us quite a scare, but he's doing a little better."

"I'm so glad. And you, Mama? Are you sure you're okay?" Rayanne released her mother.

"Darling, your mama is fine."

As Rayanne looked at her mother she was again reminded how strong she was. Rayanne greeted other family members as a nurse entered the waiting room, accompanied by Lila and Jeremy. Helen sat in the waiting room, allowing the others to spend a couple of minutes visiting Raymond in the intensive care section.

Helen and Raymond had been married nearly forty-two years, and although they were strong, proud parents, with only a high school education, they were bound and determined to see that each of their children received a decent education.

"That is something nobody can take away from ya," Rayanne remembered both of her parents saying. "A good education can open doors for ya, allow ya to be able to do things you never thought you could do. Always remember that."

Raymond's vital signs were improving. Although the prognosis was good and everyone was optimistic that he'd recover fully, Rayanne was worried and the rest of the day went by as though she were underwater. She remembered her father being seriously ill only once when he had pneumonia. She was only seven at the time, but she could tell by the look on the faces of her relatives and the hush that covered the room when she entered the house that her father's condition wasn't good.

Rayanne entered a room filled with flowers, and at the sight of her father, she felt something deep in her chest hurt. He looked so weak, so vulnerable. She looked away quickly after making eye contact with her father, blinking back the tears.

"We ain't gonna have none of that," Raymond said, opening his arms to his daughter.

Rayanne smiled and walked over to the bed to embrace her father.

"Oh, Daddy," she said, burying her face in his chest. She lifted her head and looked into his eyes. "How are you doing?"

"I reckon I went and overdid it," he said weakly.

"You always do, God only knows why," Rayanne said, and embraced her father again. "How are you feeling?"

"I'm feeling all right now, baby girl."

"Can I get you anything? A little water or something?"

"No, I don't want a thing. I'm all right now," Raymond said, smiling.

"Okay," Rayanne said, forcing a smile as well.

As Rayanne looked into the face of the man she loved more than her own life, she thought how proud she was to be his daughter. She looked into her father's face and saw lines marking the stretch of time, and it suddenly dawned on her that her parents weren't as young as they used to be. How silly could she have been? Did she think she was getting older but the rest of the world wasn't?

As Rayanne sat on the side of her father's bed, she was seeing him as she'd never seen him before. She remembered how very frightened and worried she was all those years ago when he was sick, and she was very frightened and worried now.

Chapter 18

"Daddy doesn't look good," Rayanne commented as she and Lila sat across from each other having coffee in the hospital cafeteria.

"Daddy is sick, Rayanne, he just suffered a heart attack. How do you expect him to look?" Lila replied.

"I don't know. It's been so long since I've seen him look so helpless," Rayanne said of the man who had always represented strength to her. A superhuman, in her eyes, her childhood hero, and in her heart, she was still Daddy's little girl.

"People are going to get sick, Rayanne, it happens, and Daddy is no exception. It's a part of life, but he's going to be fine, I'm sure," Lila said. Rayanne was quiet. She'd always thought that her father worked too hard, he worried too much, and the words *rest* and *exercise* were not in his vocabulary. "Don't go thinking anything negative, because if you do, Mama will pick up on it and the last thing we need is to have both of them sick."

Rayanne knew Lila was right. Their mother did appear to have a sixth sense. While they were growing up, there wasn't a thing they could get away with.

Lila was the oldest of the girls and the second to the oldest child. She was a headstrong, complicated woman whose business acumen was strong, but her personal life was always in shambles. More than ten years ago, Lila began work in an agency as a Medicare supervisor. She created, developed, and implemented programs for her agency, for which she received promotions and awards.

She'd made some smart business investments, which allowed her to acquire a substantial amount of property in South Carolina, and when she divorced Perry, she hit him hard for child support, adding to her already sizeable bank account.

Lila had further demonstrated her greed for money and power when she quietly pulled some strings and got herself on public assistance, thereby receiving a hefty check each month. As the saying goes, everything she touched turned to gold.

She played the numbers, and hit on occasions. She was becoming more financially able year after year. What she lacked, though, was compassion. There were times when Rayanne didn't know whether Lila was schizophrenic or just plain crazy. Perhaps both, Rayanne thought, but she asked, "How is Jeremy doing in school now?"

"He's doing much better since I put a belt to that ass last month," Lila answered.

"You whipped him?"

"Yes, I strapped his ass big time and why shouldn't I?"

Although Rayanne believed the adage "spare the rod and spoil the child," Lila wasn't guilty of that. Rayanne only wished that she would communicate with Jeremy some way other than with a belt. "I'm a little fuzzy on something," Rayanne said.

"Now, why doesn't that surprise me?" Lila said with a hint of sarcasm.

"You might get better results by talking to him. He's a teenager, Lila."

"He's also my son, and he's got a hard head. The boy doesn't listen."

"He's probably going through a difficult period right now, but that'll pass."

"And, another thing," Lila said, ignoring Rayanne, "He's girl crazy. That's what it is. The boy is girl crazy."

"Jeremy is thirteen years old."

"Yeah, thirteen going on thirty."

"Which teenage boy isn't crazy about girls, unless he's got some sort of problem? He's just a typical, red-blooded American boy with the same ideas and challenges as any other kid his age."

"You got that right, but check this out. I came home from work a couple of weeks ago and instead of him being at the next door neighbor's house where he was supposed to be, I found him up in the apartment with some little gal. I don't have to tell you what I found, do I?" Lila asked.

Rayanne was trying not to appear shocked. "Hell, at the rate he's going, I'll be a goddamn grandma long before I'm forty." She hadn't thought of Jeremy being sexually involved at this stage in his life.

"You know, that boy is fucking, and he doesn't even have pubic hair yet," Lila declared.

"What does one thing have to do with the other?" Rayanne asked.

"What kind of a question is that?" Lila fired back, raising her voice to the point that the people at the next table turned to look in her direction.

"What I meant, Lila, was how do you know that?"

"What? That he is fucking or that he doesn't have pubic hair?"

"Pubic hair. Actually, I suppose the other must've been pretty obvious."

"What are you talking about?" Lila asked.

"Nothing, Lila. To be honest, I don't even know why I said that." Rayanne knew from past experience that it didn't take much to set Lila off, so she changed the subject. "I wonder how long they'll keep Daddy here."

"Probably just a few days. You know Daddy. He's a toughie. He'll be back on his feet in no time."

"I hope so."

"Daddy will be out of here in no time. Hell, it'll take more than a couple of doctors to keep him away from Mama more than a few days." Lila tried to reassure her sister. "Daddy can be pretty feisty when he wants to be." Rayanne smiled weakly, but she had to agree.

Soon, though, Lila returned to the subject of Jeremy. "I don't know what I'm going to do about Jeremy. His head is so hard, he won't listen. I'm just afraid that he's going to get himself into something awful out there in those streets. New York is just not the place for him. He's trying to keep up with the street life, you know, with what's going on out there, and to tell you the truth, it isn't good. He's getting involved with things that he doesn't even begin to understand. He's losing the battle, Rayanne, and I'm afraid he's losing miserably."

"What are you going to do?"

"I really don't know," Lila sighed.

"You know you can always move back here," Rayanne offered.

"Who? Me? Move back here?"

"Yes."

"Where did you get such an idea? Why would I want to do something like that?"

"Lila, you just said you don't like Jeremy living in New York. Well, the pace here is slower, you'd be better able to keep an eye on his activities, and most of the family is here, and I'm sure they would help look after him."

"I certainly wasn't thinking about moving back here. At least, not yet."

"Exactly when were you thinking of doing it?"

According to Lila, Jeremy was growing up fast, and chances are he wasn't going to put his life on hold to wait for his mother to do something. Lila had better take charge of this situation before it got too far out of control.

"There must be some other option."

"Think about it. The change might be good for both of you."

"My God, Rayanne, be realistic. That's just about the last thing I would want to do. Besides, my life is in New York. What would I do back here?"

"You could be giving your son a chance to live."

Lila was smart and incredibly talented. She had resources that she hadn't even tapped into yet. She had money, power, and prestige where she was employed, and those things were seductive and satisfying, but she could move here, reestablish herself, and help her son to get his life back on track. Lila had enough resources that she could take whatever time was necessary to improve her life and that of her child. At some point, she could set up some sort of business and do very well.

"That's an idea, Rayanne, and I'll shelve it for

later, but what do I do right now? I need help with that boy now."

"Lila, I'll do whatever I can to help."

"Rayanne, I can hardly believe what these kids are into, what's going on in their minds today," Lila said. "It's shocking."

Rayanne understood Lila's concerns, but Rayanne also thought that a part of the problem was that a lot of the kids didn't look like kids, they didn't act like kids and they certainly didn't think like kids. Most of them wanted to be grown without being capable of accepting responsibilities as an adult. Jeremy for instance. Anyone who didn't know Jeremy wouldn't think he was only thirteen years old. Jeremy probably didn't think he was thirteen.

"Well then, sister, I think you'd better get your priorities in order. Jeremy is a kid inside a man's body. He is going to love these little girls, and they are going to love him right back, and no matter how we preach abstinence, kids are going to have sex and we are going to have to deal with it."

"All I know is that I don't want that boy climbing his little ass up on top of some little gal, thinking he knows what he's doing, when he doesn't, and getting himself in trouble. I don't need any crap like that. And another thing, I don't intend to pay no damn child support to anybody. Hell, with the economy being what it is today, I can hardly afford to take care of Jeremy and myself."

Rayanne had to laugh. "Who are you trying to kid? You have money up to your behind, so money isn't a problem."

"That's not the point, Little Miss Fort Knox. Do you realize how much it takes to raise a child? And everything that Jeremy wants costs like hell. He doesn't want anything generic. Oh no, it the real thing for Jeremy. It's designer this, designer that."

"I know that. I was joking," Rayanne said half-heartedly.

"I don't joke when it comes to my money, and it is mine, and *mine* is the operative word here. I worked hard for it, and I don't intend to support half of New York. Those young gals take their little fast asses out there, get a little piece, enjoy the hell out of it, and they go back for more. I reckon some of them see where more got them. The same place it got me," Lila said, remembering when she got pregnant with Jeremy and how she and Perry didn't get married until she was in her eighth month. She'd never forgiven Perry for delaying their nuptials and she'd never forgotten it either.

"Lila, I understand what you're saying. I get it, but what I'm talking about is worse than getting some little girl pregnant. I'm not trying to minimize teenage pregnancy. It's a growing concern in this country. What I'm saying is that some of these kids' little hormones are on fire, so we've got to keep the lines of communication open, get into their minds, listen to what they are saying, talk with them, and hope they'll listen. We can't give up on them. We've got to keep trying to do whatever it takes to reach them. We also have to talk about practicing safe sex. I hope I'm not sounding as though I'm saying these kids are bad and all they want to do is have sex, because I don't mean it that way. I'm not condoning sex either, but we should make them aware that there are alternatives. We shouldn't overlook anything. They need to know that if they're going to have sex, they should exercise some responsibility and protect themselves and their partners."

Lila had a worried look on her face, but she didn't say anything.

"Lila, we are the adults. Kids don't come with instructions. We have to work with them, teach them, guide them. We can't depend on anyone else to do the job for us."

"Yeah, right," Lila said sarcastically.

"I'm serious. This is nothing to play around with."

"I know and while we're talking, let's keep in mind that these are kids we're talking about."

"I'm not losing sight of that. Why do you think I'm so concerned? The situation would be a little less frightening if we were talking about adults. It's the kids that I'm mostly concerned about and it's up to us to try to mold them and guide them because they're the ones who aren't going to be using their heads when they meet some young fine thing."

"They'll be using their heads all right. Only it won't be the ones up top."

"It's a job, it's not going to be easy, and although we may not like the options that are available to us, we have to make choices. We have to do what's best for the children. We have to do what's in their best interest."

"I have no intention of moving back home right now, if that's where you're going again. There's got to be another answer." Lila paused a moment. "I wonder whether John and Christen would let Jeremy stay with them for a while."

"What?"

John was the second oldest brother. He'd met and married Christen after they graduated from college seven years ago, and although they wanted children very much and according to them, it wasn't due to lack of trying, Christen didn't conceive. That had been a big part of the problem, causing her to turn heavily to alcohol.

Christen was a good person, you couldn't ask for a better sister-in-law, but there were times when she was moody as hell. John, an assistant principal, and Christen, who worked in the school system as well, lived in a three-bedroom, ranch-style home. The entire house was beautifully furnished, with the exception of one room that was left empty with the hope of one day making it into a nursery.

"I wonder if they would take Jeremy in."

Rayanne had been taken aback by that suggestion. "Did you talk with them about this last year?"

"Yeah, but Christen wasn't too happy about it, and you know John. He is only going to do what Christen wants. Would you talk with them for me? Christen likes you. I think they'd do it if you asked them."

"This is something that you need to take care of."

"Well, correct me if I'm wrong, Miss Thang, but I thought you wanted to help."

"I said I'd do what I could to help," Rayanne corrected.

"You are so damn selfish. You are so caught up in your own little world that you are not willing to lift a finger to help anybody else."

"That's not true and you know it. You are just pissed because I won't ask John and Christen to raise your son when he has a healthy, living, breathing mother and father who are capable of doing the job themselves," Rayanne said. "I am sorry, Lila, but I don't think John and Christen are the answer to the problem. You have got to decide what's best for your son. I can't find a home for Jeremy, but I will help if you can come up with a viable solution. Lila, if you spent less time trying to become the wealthiest person in New York and more time being a mother, you might not be having these problems." Rayanne knew Lila didn't like what she was saying, but she continued. "Sometimes we can't have it all when we have children. We have to give up something, make sacrifices. Kids are wonderful, but we have got to spend time with them. Think about it, Lila. We have got to remember that time is not a renewable resource. We can't replace it or make it up in any way when it's gone. Another thing, we certainly can't pass our children off on someone else when trouble comes."

"Where do you get off at saying something like that? It's not like that and you know it. John has been telling Mama and Daddy how much they want children."

"They want a baby," Rayanne said. "There's a difference in having their own baby and having someone else's half-grown child. It just isn't the same."

"Don't get damn technical with me."

"Look, Lila." Rayanne threw up her hands in exasperation. "You talk with John and Christen and if you all can work it out, the problem will be solved."

Lila was quiet but Rayanne knew her mind was at work. Lila's mind was always at work. "If Christen was any damn good, she would have given my brother kids a long time ago," she said.

"I wouldn't go there."

"And why the hell not?"

"Because you don't know why they haven't had kids."

"John is a Wilson and us Wilsons are fertile

people. We are full of babies." Lila paused a moment and looked at Rayanne. "Hell, I thought you would have had at least one by now," she said. "It's not like you haven't been having your little house painted." Lila changed the subject. "By the way, did you bring that fine-ass Ralph home with you?"

Lila had met Ralph only once when Rayanne invited her to a play, but she remembered him all too well.

"No, I didn't," Rayanne answered.

"I would never have left something that good looking back in New York. That brother is fine."

"What do you expect me to do? Carry him around in my pocket?"

"I would," Lila laughed. She shrugged her shoulders and said, "You asked, so I'm telling you." Rayanne didn't comment. "You will learn sooner or later, little sister, that you can't trust these men, especially the fine ones," Lila said bitterly.

"Ralph and I wouldn't have much of a relationship if we didn't trust each other."

"A word to the wise," Lila said, with a smirk on her face.

Why was it that Lila always thought that she knew a little bit more than anyone else, about everything? Rayanne wondered.

"I know what you are thinking," Lila said. "You're thinking that I think I'm right. It's not that, Rayanne. I just don't want to see you get hurt."

"That's the last thing you need to be thinking about right now."

"I am just saying be careful who you trust."

"There's an element of risk in most things," Rayanne said, nonchalant.

"The eternal optimist."

"Lila, I'm not stupid, but I'm also not going to live my life worrying about what some man is doing when we're not together."

"Some man? I thought Ralph meant more to you than that."

"Ralph means a great deal to me. I am in love with him and he loves me," Rayanne said and threw up her hands. "How'd this conversation get turned around to me anyway? I thought we were talking about Jeremy."

"I get that you are in love with Ralph. I'm just saying don't put too much trust in one man. Who trusted anyone more than I trusted Perry? And look where it got me. You see what he did to me," Lila said, but Rayanne was thinking that perhaps she asked for what she got. "Perry got tired of me, he split, and that's all there was to it."

"I don't know that it's any one person's fault when a marriage fails," Rayanne said.

"It was all his fault. I did everything for the man, and he walked off and left me for some old-ass broad. The bitch is almost as old as Mama."

"I don't think age had anything to do with it," Rayanne replied.

"Obviously," Lila said. Everyone in the family thought it was uncharacteristic of Perry's behavior to just walk out like he did, but they also knew that Lila stayed on his back. And, as for trusting him, she was always suspicious, even when there was no reason to be. She'd made the man miserable, but Rayanne didn't think that Perry ever stopped loving Lila. She simply made it impossible for him to live with her. If she'd only thought to put his happiness before her own insecurities, she would've been pleased with the dividends, and Rayanne had told her as much.

The two women sat quietly for a moment. Lila needed time to formulate her thoughts, to reflect on what Rayanne had said. Once she accomplished her goal, she said, "So, little sister is teaching big sister the facts of life." Rayanne smiled, but she didn't say anything. Lila looked up to see Rayanne looking at her, and she smiled. "What?" Lila asked.

"I was just thinking."

"About what?"

"You and how you went about preparing for Jeremy when you were pregnant. You read all the books on babies, painted the nursery and crib yellow, bought records of the sound of rain and the ocean and played them while carrying him and after he was born, to keep him calm and peaceful, which I might add, was great. You're quite a woman when you want to be."

Lila looked at Rayanne and smiled. "That's quite a compliment."

"Well, it's true, but that's only when you"—Rayanne pointed a finger at Lila—"want to be."

They laughed together, and this was a rare occasion for the two of them to share anything, even something as simple as laughter. But laughing was good, for both of them.

John and Jeremy entered the cafeteria and joined the women at their table. "Wad up, Mom, Aunt Rayanne?" Jeremy leaned over to give Rayanne a hug and a kiss on the cheek.

"Hey, Jeremy."

"What did I tell you about talking like that? What does wad up mean?" Lila threw at her son. "Where do you think you are going to get in life talking like that?"

"What have you been up to, Jeremy?" Rayanne ran her arm affectionately around his shoulders.

"Just hanging out with Uncle John," Jeremy answered.

"You're not giving Uncle John and Auntie Christen a hard time, are you?" Lila asked.

"No, Mom." Jeremy wrinkled his nose.

"Jeremy is a good kid," John said, sitting down and resting his arms on the table. "I thought the two of you were going home."

"We were, but we stopped off here for coffee," Lila answered.

"How was Daddy when you left him?" Rayanne asked, the crease back in her forehead.

"He seemed to be holding his own," John answered.

"And Mama?" she asked.

"I was finally able to talk her into going home and getting some rest," he said.

"Good. She's been here since Daddy was brought in," Rayanne said.

"Yeah, but she's okay. You know Mama," John said. "She's a rock."

"She's upset about Daddy, but Mama is fine," Lila agreed.

"Maxine is driving her home and she'll stay with her until you get there," John said.

"Maxine looks fantastic," Lila said, changing the subject.

"She does," Rayanne agreed. "She's looking like her old self again."

Maxine was the sister between Lila and Rayanne. She was short, pretty, and shapely. She was a lab technician at the hospital. Her marriage to Fred Duncan, a plumbing contractor, had produced two sons, Bobby and Bruce. The marriage had been good. She was made to feel special. She was an equal partner in the decisions made in their lives. She loved Fred and felt he loved her, which was why she was devastated when Fred ran off, leaving her alone to raise the boys.

Maxine later filed for divorce, Fred didn't contest it, and their marriage of nine years was dissolved. Her devastation was short-lived, though because soon afterward, she met Marcus Richards and after a brief courtship, they married. A year and a half after that union, Maxine gave birth to a baby girl, Marcia Raylyn. Maxine and the kids realized later that when Fred left, it was the best thing that he could've happened to them.

"Maxine and the kids are fine. That Marcus is one hell of a nice guy," John said.

"That damn Fred," Lila said. "He hasn't given Maxine any support for the boys or herself since he left."

"I don't think Maxine wants anything for herself, but surely Fred should be doing something for the boys," Rayanne said.

"It's not as if he can't afford to," Lila said. "The man was a shit contractor, for heaven's sake, and he made a lot of money back then. He is a resourceful man, so I am sure that he is doing all right."

"Plumbing contractor," John attempted to correct her.

"I know what he does," Lila spat out. "But the point is he made good money then, and I'm sure he still does. Like I said, Fred is resourceful. He has always had a knack for making money, so I'll bet he's got plenty. Another thing, whatever went on between him and Maxine was one thing, but to neglect his children, now, that is wrong," Lila said, and Rayanne agreed. "I don't know what some of these men are using for brains. Hell, we don't make these babies alone. Oh, they are there for the making but not the finish. It takes a real man to hang in there for the long haul."

"We're not that bad." John smiled.

"Speak for yourself," Lila said.

"I am," John said.

"Look at the record here. Perry and I got married, had a baby, we got divorced. Maxine and Fred got married, had two babies, they got divorced. Two out of two marriages of your sisters failed and we weren't at fault. What do you say to that?" Lila said, not giving John an opportunity to respond. "These guys just walked off without a word." Lila turned her attention to Rayanne. "I wouldn't rush into it if I were you. Look around, have a good time, but put off getting married for a while," she said.

"At least Perry didn't drop the ball. He takes care of his son," John said, winking at Jeremy, who smiled and returned the wink. Then to Rayanne, "Don't let her scare you off, baby. Marriage, like anything you really want, takes work. There are some bad apples out there, but that goes both ways."

"You know most of you guys are full of it. You can't be trusted. Irresponsible jackasses," Lila muttered.

"Who are we talking about?" John asked.

"I'm just talking in general," Lila answered.

"Well, don't worry about Maxine. She's good, happy as can be," John assured them.

"That girl hit the jackpot the second time around."

"Marcus is a good man," John said. "And it's great how he relates to all of them, especially the boys. They are a family now, and it's plain to see that the kids are crazy about him."

"Mom, give me a couple of dollars," Jeremy said, interrupting their conversation.

"What do you want a couple of dollars for, and is that any way to ask?" Lila asked.

"I'm sorry, Mom. May I have a few dollars, please?" Jeremy rephrased the question. "I want to get a soda and a candy bar."

"When you can't ask for things any better than that, young man, you need to have a job and your own money," Lila said, handing the boy a ten-dollar bill. Jeremy thanked her and rushed over to make a purchase. "That boy," she said.

"Give the kid a break, Lila," John said.

"I don't want Jeremy growing up thinking he can get anything he wants, anytime he wants it, and he needs to have better manners. A kid without manners is something to deal with. He will grow up being a jerk. Speaking of jerks," Lila said, "does anyone know where Fred is now? Maxine said the last she'd heard, he was in Florida or was it Georgia? I don't know, but he's the most exasperating man that I know."

Rayanne tried not to be judgmental, but Fred was high on her list of exasperating men as well.

"Well, good riddance to him," Lila said.

"Mama said Daddy likes Marcus also," Rayanne

said, wringing her hands, and John reached out and took one of her hands into his.

"I know you're worried about Daddy, sweetheart, we all are, but we've got to hang in there for both of our parents," John said.

"That's what I've been telling her," Lila said, and suddenly she was distracted.

John and Rayanne saw who had captured their sister's attention. "This woman will never change," John laughed.

"Who is that man?" Lila asked.

"That's Larry," John replied.

"You know that wonderful specimen?" Lila asked, never taking her eyes off the handsome stranger.

"Yeah, we play ball together," John answered. He and Larry had hung out on occasion and had gone on fishing trips. "Larry's a nice guy."

"Well, introduce me," Lila ordered.

"I can, but just so you know, he's married and has two precious little girls," John said.

"John, I didn't ask for his résumé and I am not in the market for a husband at the moment, I just asked to be introduced to the man."

John waved to Larry and he came over to the table.

Larry was handsome, well built, and moved with the grace of an athlete when he approached them.

"What's up, Larry?" John got up and shook Larry's hand. "Larry, these are my sisters, Rayanne and Lila. Girls, this is Larry."

Jeremy returned and John finished the introduction. "And this is Lila's son, Jeremy."

Larry shook Jeremy's hand also.

"Pleased to meet y'all," Larry said. "I hope the

reason you all are here is nothing too serious." He looked from one face to the other.

"Daddy had a heart attack," John explained.

"I didn't know that, man. I'm sorry," Larry said. "How's he doing?"

"He seems to be doing pretty good," Lila said.

"Let me know if there's anything I can do," Larry said.

"Just good thoughts and prayers," John said.

"You got it," Larry said.

"What are you doing here? Is everything all right with you and your family?" John asked.

"Yeah, everything's fine. I had to get a physical for the job." He looked at his watch. "So I reckon I had better be getting on back."

"Okay, Larry. Good seeing you, man. Take care," John said.

"You too, and hang in there," Larry said, extending his hand to John.

"It was nice meeting y'all," he said to Lila and Rayanne. "You too, my man," he said to Jeremy. "I hope the next time we meet it won't be under similar circumstances." Then he left.

"A nice man," Lila said.

"A married man," John reminded her.

"I got it," Lila said, annoyed. "And thank you, John, for not referring to me as your oldest sister. That's the first time you introduced me and didn't say, 'This is my oldest sister, Lila.' I was so sick of you always doing that to me." Lila and John laughed. Rayanne's mind was elsewhere. "Rayanne, would you loosen up?" Lila said.

Rayanne looked from Lila's face to John's. How could she explain how she was feeling? How could she relay her thoughts and fears without bringing everyone down? Her father was in his late sixties and he was ill, and to Rayanne he seemed very different, so unlike his usual self. Rayanne had always been a person of divine faith and a positive thinker, but she knew that life could change drastically, within a split second, and at that moment, she felt helpless, wondering whether her father would ever be the same again.

Chapter 19

Although only three and a half miles separated the hospital and the family house, the drive seemed much longer. At first, Lila couldn't shut up about Larry and what a nice man he was. When she said she wondered what it would be like to date him, Rayanne reminded her that not only did the man have a living, breathing wife, but he had two children as well. They rode the rest of the way in silence with Lila sporting a secretive smile. Rayanne didn't have to ask to know exactly what was on her mind. The same as always. Men. And this time, Larry Jacobs.

Rayanne pulled into the driveway and stopped the car. She unhooked her seat belt and sat for a moment to take in the beauty of the yard. It was picturesque, colorful. It was a place of beauty. Her mother had spent a lot of time working in the yard, making sure that there would always be colorful flowers, and sure enough, the yard held a burst of colors year-round.

Mostly chrysanthemums lined the edge of the yard on either side of the house. A sprinkling of zinnias were still evident as well as other fall and winter flowering plants. Her favorite flowers that bloomed in early spring, which she missed most because she didn't spend much time home during that time of year, were the azaleas and the white dogwood trees. The lawn that was freshly cut and still green held a mother duck and three babies that sat on the lawn near the white bird bath that stood in the center of the front yard.

Lila had already gotten out of the car and was standing on the porch, looking impatient, by the time Rayanne removed her bags from the trunk. Rayanne set her bags onto the driveway, walked across the lawn, and picked up the paper. She tucked it under her arm and used her old key to let herself and Lila in.

Rayanne stood on the threshold and took in the view. Their home had been remodeled since all the kids had grown up and left home. Where there were four bedrooms, a living room, and a kitchen that doubled as a dining room, the house now had only three bedrooms, but a formal dining room and a large family room were added. The furniture was old but still in good taste and the house was immaculate. Helen always kept it that way, and as the saying goes, you could eat off the floors in her home.

Rayanne and her siblings were blessed with parents who had an enormous capacity to love, and that love was not limited to family and close friends; they showered their love on anyone who'd accept it. When Rayanne and Ivory brought Dorian home for a visit, Dorian was adopted by each family. They fell in love with her, and she them. Dorian still didn't talk much about her own family, so her past was still something of a mystery, but she made a quick connection with Helen and had promised to visit as often as she could. And, in doing so, she and Helen became close and Dorian shared more with Helen than she did anyone.

"If you're not going in, would you move aside and let me?" Lila's words pulled Rayanne from her reverie.

They entered the house. Helen had set the tables in the dining room and the kitchen, because when the entire family gathered, one table wasn't enough to accommodate them all.

The house was filled with wonderful odors of food. Rayanne had managed to keep her figure during the years. She was a trim five feet seven inches, but her mind had already begun to calculate the calories and the pounds that would settle in some unwanted place on her body, if she weren't careful, as she eyed the food on the stove. Her stomach would have no choice, she thought as the smells invaded her nostrils. "Mama," Rayanne called out. "You're cooking?"

"Yeah, some of everybody's favorites," she answered, stirring the collards.

"I thought you came home to get some rest," Rayanne said, noticing that the sleepless nights her mother had recently gone through showed on her face, yet she moved about the kitchen with what appeared to be untouched energy.

"Honey, I ain't done a thing but cooked a little something," Helen said.

"A little something," Rayanne said.

Mama had gone all out, Rayanne thought. Helen had two chickens roasting with stuffing in the oven. She was making collards, browned rice, black-eyed peas, candied yams, peach cobbler, and corn bread.

There was even a slab of ribs cooking in the oven. This was no feat for Helen. This meal wasn't even to compare with one of her Sunday dinners when all the children were still at home. She'd prepared almost twice that amount of food on Sunday mornings when the children were growing up, and she'd be fresh as a daisy, teaching her Sunday school class at nine thirty every Sunday morning.

"I wish you wouldn't push yourself this way. There are enough of us around to take care of the meals." Helen heard her daughter, but she didn't mend her pace, finishing up what she was doing.

"If you wanna make yourself useful," Helen said to Rayanne, "make another picture of tea. I need to pull them ribs out of the oven. And, Lila, you put another water pitcher and some glasses on the tables."

"Yes, ma'am," Lila said playfully, but she did as she was told.

Within an hour, everyone gathered around the large dining table where Helen asked the blessings before they were seated at both tables to eat. Helen always felt that a family should eat at least one meal together every day, even if only for a half hour. It kept families together, she thought.

Although Rayanne hadn't eaten since she munched over an egg salad sandwich and a soda for lunch in the hospital cafeteria, and the smell in the kitchen made her mouth water, she toyed with the food and realized she was no longer hungry, once it was on her plate.

After dinner, she excused herself and went into her bedroom to call Ralph. She was a little surprised that he hadn't phoned her. She flipped the switch that flooded her bedroom with light, which poured from a hand-cut crystal with brass-plated base lamps. The rose-pink comforter and shams were simple elegance and the pink organdy matching sheers and tie-back drapes cast a soft spell across the room. She dialed his number, got his machine, and left a message.

When Rayanne returned to the hospital that evening, it was difficult, but she was successful in convincing her mother to stay home that night. Rayanne was surprised at how much her daddy seemed to have improved from when she'd seen him earlier. She was happy, so much so that she found herself humming to a tune that played on the car radio on her way home that night.

Everyone had gone to bed except Helen and Lila, who were sitting at the kitchen table. Rayanne informed them of Raymond's improved condition. Then she asked her mother, "What about Josh, Mama? How is he?"

"You know Josh," Helen said. "Still drinking like a fish."

"Is he, Mama?"

Rayanne and Josh were the youngest of the siblings and they'd been very close growing up. Josh had earned a degree in engineering at Clemson, but he didn't put it to much use most of the time because of his drinking. However, he'd managed to hold on to his most recent job at the power plant in Georgia. Josh was smart. He'd been an honor student from his sophomore year until he graduated from college, but as they say, women and alcohol can destroy a good man. In Josh's case, it was the latter.

"Yeah, your daddy and I done talk to him until we're just about blue in the face, but it don't seem to do no good," Helen said sadly.

Rayanne knew Josh was an alcoholic, although he'd never admit it. She also knew all too well that alcoholics rarely admit that they are.

"He needs help, Mama," Rayanne said, a frown creasing her forehead. She heard Lila clicking her teeth and was about to leave the room.

"You turning in?" Helen asked Lila.

"I may go out for a while. I'm not sure yet," Lila said as she left the room.

Helen nodded and gave a half smile, then said to Rayanne, "You're right about Josh, and we're trying, but it's hard."

"I know," Rayanne said, looking thoughtful.

Helen reached across the kitchen table and rubbed Rayanne's hand. "Don't you worry yourself about Josh. He's gonna get the help he needs. Me and your daddy are gonna see to that. And get that buckle outta your brow. If you don't, you're gonna look old before your time."

Rayanne smiled and said, "You always say that."

"I know because it's true." Helen grinned.

"What about Beverly?" Rayanne asked.

"She's fine until Josh gets on her nerves. Then, it's a merry-go-round. One week she's there, the next she's gone," Helen said, shaking her head.

When the microwave turned off, Helen got up and removed a plate of spare ribs, rice and collards and set it on the table in front of Rayanne. "I put a little something aside for you, seeing you didn't eat much dinner."

"Mama, you didn't have to do that," Rayanne said, getting up from the table.

Helen was about to pour a glass of iced tea, but Rayanne took the glass from her hand and poured it herself. "Here, I'll take that. Now, you sit right here." Rayanne pulled out a chair at the table and stood behind it until her mother sat down. "You are too good to us, Mama."

"I don't mind, honey."

"I know and I hope you and Daddy know that we appreciate everything you do for us," Rayanne said, and her mother smiled and nodded her head.

Rayanne poured a glass of tea from the pitcher. "Can I get you a glass of tea, Mama?" she asked.

"No, baby, I don't want nothin' else tonight," Helen said.

Rayanne sat back at the table. She took a sip from the tea glass and returned to their earlier conversation. "Beverly is a good girl, and I can't say I blame her when she splits on Josh when it becomes unbearable. Living with a drunk is no picnic," Rayanne said, stuffing a fork of collards and rice into her mouth.

"I know it. Shucks, Josh is my son and I love him dearly, but sometimes he comes in here so sloppy drunk that I want to walk right out and give him the house," Helen said, looking at Rayanne.

She wiped her mouth with a paper napkin Helen had put on the table beside her plate. "Sure Mama, that will be the day when you turn away from any of your children for any reason," Rayanne snickered.

Helen grinned as well. "Josh isn't all bad. He's as nice as can be, he is as smart as a whip and could be doing so much more with his self, but that drinking, Lordy, Lordy." Helen smiled and shook her head. "But we're gonna do the best we can, and leave the rest in the hands of the Lord and let His will be done. You know, honey, we don't get to pick out the kind of families that we get no more than we can clean up germs," Helen said, and Rayanne knew her mother had never uttered truer words.

Rayanne pushed her plate away and took another sip of tea.

"What else is bothering you, baby? I know you're worrying 'bout your daddy and Josh, but something else seems to be troubling you," Helen said.

Helen always seemed to know when something was going on with her children. Rayanne didn't want to tell her what was bothering her, but she didn't want to lie either. She looked at her mother. "I was thinking about Dorian."

"What about Dorian?" Helen asked.

"Dorian has a drug problem," Rayanne said, and she didn't stop talking until she'd told Helen everything.

"I don't know why she wants to do a fool thing like that, and such a pretty girl. Lord have mercy," Helen whispered. "Well, honey, we just gotta be there for her. It's hard to help when the people you want to help don't want it. We still gotta let 'em know we love 'em and that what they're doing is not just hurting them, but it's hurting all of us who love them. And we gotta pray. That's the most important thing."

Rayanne felt much better after they talked and she thought how much she was going to miss her mother when she returned to New York.

Lila hung up the phone and entered the family room wearing a long blushing-pink nightgown with matching robe and slippers. She had her long black hair pulled back and twisted into a ball at the back of her head. Although Lila was a little on the plump side, she was very attractive and very much aware of the effect she had on men.

"What are you two talking about?" she asked, and without waiting for an answer, she walked out onto the side porch, closing the door behind her.

Helen looked at Rayanne, shrugged her shoulders, and smiled. "Oh, honey, I forgot to tell you that Ralph called while you were at the hospital. Said he was gonna call you back." The phone rang again and Lila rushed in and scooped it up.

"Hello," she said in her sexiest voice. She looked at Rayanne, handed the phone to her, and returned to the porch. It was Maxine.

The phone beeped during their conversation and when Rayanne answered, it was Ralph calling back. She quickly ended the call with her sister, promising to call her back, and she talked with Ralph. She was excited. She'd seen him less than twenty-four hours ago, but it seemed an eternity. She'd missed Ralph and told him so.

"I miss you too, baby," he said and asked, "How is your father?"

"He's improving. He looked even better tonight when I saw him."

"I'm glad. Now, when are you coming back here?"

"Sounds like someone misses me."

Ralph had become so much a part of Rayanne's life for so long now that she could hardly remember what it was like before they met.

"You got that right."

"Well, I'm not sure, honey. It depends on how well Daddy gets along." Rayanne relayed a good night to Ralph from her mother, who waved to her as she left the room.

"So I've got you all to myself now," Ralph said.

"I'm afraid so," Rayanne chuckled.

"Well, I hope all goes well so you can hurry back here to me, because I just couldn't handle living in this big city without you much longer."

Feeling warm and tingly all over, Rayanne made a suggestion. "Why don't you think about coming down for a few days?" she asked. "It would be great if you got away from the city and came down for the weekend. The family would love seeing you again."

"I may just do that," he said, "because this loneliness ain't happening."

They talked a half hour more and then Rayanne hung up and went to bed.

Dorian and Ivory flew down to South Carolina, and Dorian spent a lot of time talking with Helen. She was always easy to talk with. Even when Rayanne was in high school, her friends sometimes came over just to talk with Helen. But as it turned out, Ralph never did make the trip.

After spending a couple of days in South Carolina, Rayanne drove Ivory and Dorian to the airport and upon returning home, she visited her Aunt Bessie. Although Aunt Bessie was in her late seventies, her faculties hadn't been dulled by age and she was still one of the feistiest women Rayanne knew.

Rayanne spent a week at home after her daddy was released from the hospital. She spent a lot of time talking with her parents and she shopped for food to make sure the house was well stocked before she left. Although she was scheduled to return to New York the following day and it appeared her father was doing well, she was still a little skeptical about leaving.

After putting away the food she'd just bought,

she went into the den where her parents were sitting and watching TV. Helen was sitting in an easy chair not far from the chaise lounge where Raymond lay with a lightweight throw covering him from the waist down.

"Come on in here, daughter," Raymond said to Rayanne.

She kissed her parents and sat on the couch.

"What are you all watching?" Rayanne asked.

"*Oprah*," Helen answered.

"Mama, you still watch *Oprah*?"

"Yeah, I love *Oprah*," Helen said.

"She even got me watching it," Raymond said, smiling.

"Well, I'm not complaining. I watch every chance I get as well," Rayanne said.

"Daughter," her father began, and Rayanne could see from his expression that he was about to get into a serious conversation. "We been wanting to talk to you."

"Oh yeah?" Rayanne smiled adoringly at her father. "What you and Mama want to talk with me about?" she asked.

"We know you're worried 'bout me, but I'm gonna be fine," Raymond said. "We know you got some concerns 'bout going back to New York, but don't. You have a life there now and you need to go back to it. Sure, we wish you could be here all the time, but we know how you feel about New York, the work you do and your life back there. We raised you to follow your heart, be true to yourself, not to hide out here at home. You done all you can do here. Now you gotta go on and live your life and, baby, do it with our blessings."

"That's right, honey, you go on back and if we

need you, we'll call. You know that, but we're gon' be just fine and besides, Raymond and I got each other." Helen reached over and caught her husband's hand and they smiled at each other.

"So you are kicking me out?" Rayanne teased her parents.

"We ain't never gon' do that, but you are young and we want you to live your life. Honey, your daddy and I done lived and enjoyed our lives more than you'll ever imagine," Helen said, "And we're gon' have some more good times."

Rayanne looked at her parents and smiled as tears welled up in her eyes.

The night before her departure, she packed her suitcases and called Ralph, but got his answering machine. She didn't leave a message. When she had spoken with him the day before, she told Ralph she wasn't sure when she would be returning to New York. Her father was improving, but she would let him know later of her decision. Well, she thought, she would surprise him.

Rayanne walked out onto the front porch. She stretched her hands out against the railing that framed the porch and she watched the moon as it edged its way across the sky to mark the judgment of time. She watched as the stars twinkled, making their presence clear, and in doing so, Rayanne wondered for the first time whether the stars communicated with each other, and if they did, what did they talk about? Did they experience emotions? Did they have secrets of their own?

There was just a hint of fall chilling the air, and as Rayanne sat in the porch swing, she began to think about returning to New York. She also thought of her parents and thinking for the first time that although she missed Ralph and wanted to see him badly, she didn't want to leave her parents in spite of her earlier conversation with them.

As Rayanne sat hunched over with her arms folded across her chest on the front porch of her parents' home, she began to reflect. From that porch, she had been able to sit in the quiet and peace and settle a lot of life's problems. Many decisions about how she would pursue her future goals were made right there on that porch.

She was immersed in her thoughts, when Lila said from the door, "You all set for the trip back to New York in the morning?"

"I suppose so," Rayanne said, reservation flooding her voice. "Aunt Bessie said she was hoping to see you before we leave."

"Oh my goodness," Lila said with a groan, putting her hands up to her face. "I meant to stop by to see her. How is she?"

"She's worried about Daddy, but she's okay. She's still as sharp as ever."

Aunt Bessie was amazing. She ran her house alone, kept it immaculate, did her own banking and shopping, but got someone to drive her where she needed to go. That was the only thing that'd changed about her. She no longer drove. "I took her to the grocery store yesterday and she wouldn't even let me push the shopping cart. No, ma'am. She pushed that thing up and down those aisles herself," Rayanne chuckled. After a moment, she fell silent.

Lila noticed Rayanne's silence and said, "You still worrying about Daddy?"

"Yes, that too, but I was thinking about something

Aunt Bessie said today. She told me our cousin, Stevie, stole from her the last time he was home."

"I don't doubt it, given the situation he created for himself," Lila said. "I don't even speak to Stevie when I see him. I try to avoid him whenever I can."

"He's still family," Rayanne said.

"That's not my fault," Lila said stiffly, and Rayanne could understand her feeling that way. They knew that Stevie was using drugs and his career had gone to pot. No pun intended, but that was a fact. His career had gone down the drain. He'd literally become a bum, but blood was thicker than water.

"It breaks Aunt Bessie's heart to see her only child come to this. Uncle Steve had never gotten over the way Stevie Jr. turned out."

"Stevie Jr. is a trip and I certainly don't want him anywhere near my son. Jeremy doesn't need that kind of influence in his life." Lila sneered. "He needs to get it together with his grown behind."

"It's such a waste. Stevie is an intelligent, good-looking man who had everything going for him. It is amazing how a person can be on top of the world one day and rolling around in some gutter the next."

"It's about the choices we make."

"Yeah," Rayanne said, her voice trailing off.

"So, what were you so engrossed in when I came out here?" Lila asked, changing the subject. "It seemed like you were going through an intense moment. Like you had something heavy on your mind."

"It was nothing really."

"Don't give me that. I bet I know what—or should I say who—was occupying your mind."

"Tell me. That way, we'll both know," Rayanne said in good humor.

"Don't be flip with me. You were thinking about Ralph. I'd even go further and say you're worried about him. Hell, I would be. Your father was hospitalized after having a heart attack, you've been here two whole weeks, and he hasn't brought his ass down here once and you're supposed to be the love of his life."

"Looks like you've gone into mind reading," Rayanne said, laughing softly.

"But I'm right, aren't I?" Rayanne didn't respond. "You don't have to say, but I'm sure I'm right. Just a woman's intuition." Lila smirked and walked over to where she could face Rayanne. She leaned with her back against the railing.

"You and your woman's intuition," Rayanne said, pushing off in the swing.

"Maybe it's a little more than that." Lila smiled.

Rayanne stopped the swing abruptly and asked, "What are you getting at, Lila?"

Lila threw her hands up in the air. "Hell, never mind. If you are satisfied with the way your man treats you, then it's fine with me. It's your business, not mine."

"You could've fooled me," Rayanne said.

"I would be a little suspicious, though," Lila said, smiling wickedly at Rayanne.

Rayanne thought she'd better take this head-on or Lila wouldn't give up. She'd picked all night, trying to get a rise out of her. So unless she faced Lila and let her know under no uncertain terms that she should mind her own business, it would go on and on.

"Suspicious about what?" Rayanne said. "What

should I be suspicious about, Lila? For your information, Ralph is a man."

Lila interrupted, saying under her breath, "A foine man at that."

Rayanne ignored whatever it was that Lila mumbled. "As I was saying, Ralph is a man, he is a busy man, and aside from that, he has a life of his own. But just in case you hadn't noticed, he and I are not joined at the hip. We live independent of each other."

"Rayanne, the man hasn't bothered to put in an appearance in all this time. Are you telling me that you haven't asked yourself why at least once?" Lila sneered and it was more evident than before that her bitterness over losing Perry was turning her cruel. And even if Rayanne had wondered why Ralph hadn't made the trip, she'd never admit it to Lila.

Lila sat in the swing next to Rayanne. "If he was my man, he'd have a hell of a lot of explaining to do."

"Divorcing Perry certainly has made you bitter. Just because he walked over you doesn't mean that that's a way of life for women, because it's not. God," Rayanne said, shaking her head, "I pity the next man who gets involved with you because you're gonna kick his behind for everything Perry did and things you thought he did."

Rayanne was almost sorry she brought up Perry's name. He was a soft spot in Lila's heart. She knew Lila still loved Perry and that he'd probably always be Lila's strongest weakness, and any comment that was the slightest bit negative would hurt her, but Rayanne didn't care. She just wanted Lila to get off her back. That was her only weapon and she used it when necessary. There were lots of things on Rayanne's mind. Ralph, of course, was one, but there were her parents, and at that time, they were the ones who were uppermost in her mind.

As she thought about it, though, she looked at Lila and was about to apologize but she found Lila looking at her with clenched teeth.

"You bitch," Lila hurled. "How can you be that cruel?"

"Look, I'm sorry, but you just wouldn't let up. We're leaving here tomorrow and I'm concerned about Mama and Daddy. As far as Ralph is concerned, sure, he does some things that I question, but I don't speculate about it and make myself miserable. Ralph and I are free to do as we please, date other people if we choose to, whatever. It just happens that we don't choose to," Rayanne informed her.

"What black man is going to allow his woman to date other men if he is truly into her?" Lila asked, with raised eyebrows.

"Ralph doesn't allow me to do anything. Each of us is our own person. We make our own decisions and we control our own happenings. We don't dictate what the other can or cannot do. We are not control freaks. That's a mistake a lot of couples make." Rayanne seemed to have gotten through to Lila.

Lila sat back in the swing and crossed her legs. "Okay, if that's how you see it."

She reached into her pocket and pulled out a piece of gum, removed the wrapper, and stuck it into her mouth. "Speaking of men, I thought I would have seen some of my old friends by now."

"You know most of your old friends are married."

"Are you making a point?"

"No, just an observation."

"Rayanne, I learned a long time ago that if you don't step out and take chances, nothing will ever happen. I don't want to mess up anyone's home life. I just want to have a little fun, that's all," Lila said, but Rayanne knew nothing in life was that simple with Lila, as possessive as she was.

"You'll have some poor man flying to New York so often that he'll probably start buying stock in the airlines," Rayanne said, and Lila chuckled.

"One of my friends called earlier, but he was doubtful whether he could get out tonight. I looked up his number in the phone book and if I don't hear from him in the next half hour, I'm going to call him."

"This is not New York. This is a small town and you know how people talk."

"Who gives a damn?" Lila said. "Come go for a ride with me."

"Where are you going this time of night? You know our flight is at the crack of dawn."

"Are you coming or not?"

"Not, but be careful."

"You don't want to go, so don't worry about it."

Rayanne gave her a look.

Lila noticed and said, "Life hurts, doesn't it?"

Rayanne agreed. Lots of things in life hurt, and dating a married man could be a very painful experience. She'd known people who'd gone that route and it was a dead-end street.

"Rayanne," Lila said thoughtfully, "if I die tonight, this world wouldn't owe me a damn thing. Know why? Because I've done it all. I haven't just thought about it, I've lived, and I don't intend to stop, at least not now." Rayanne knew the type of personality that Lila had. She was possessive and clinging, and she didn't need to get involved with no man who was married. She'd make his life miserable. "It could turn out better than you think," Lila was saying. "Anyway, I won't know if I don't try, will I?"

"Hey, if that is what you want to do, then go for it," Rayanne said. Then she got up and went into the house.

From the bathroom, Rayanne heard Lila come into the house. She spoke with someone on the telephone and she left. Rayanne stepped into the shower, shampooed her hair, and rubbed her favorite soap all over her body. She blow-dried her hair, set it on a few large rollers, and went to bed. Once in bed, she had trouble sleeping. She looked at the clock on the nightstand. A quarter to one.

An hour later, she was still awake. There was a soft tap on her door. Lila poked her head into the room and switched on the light.

"I thought I was gonna have to send a posse for you," Rayanne said, blinking under the light.

Lila smiled wickedly. "Is Jeremy here?"

"It's a fine time to ask," Rayanne said, shielding her eyes from the light with her hand.

"Is he here or not?" Lila asked, losing patience.

"He's here. Maxine and Marcus brought him shortly after you left."

"Good. I'll see you in the morning, then," Lila said, flipped the light off, and closed the door.

Rayanne turned over in bed and before long, she was awakened to the soft buzz of the alarm clock. Within a few hours, she would have returned to the rustle and bustle of the fastest-moving city in the world, and her life there, the life she'd loved so much, but she knew before returning this time that it wouldn't be the same.

Chapter 20

Rayanne went through a heap of mail that Yvonne had piled on the desk, and although her accountant took care of most of her bills, she still wrote checks to cover the underground parking space where she kept her new black Corvette, and she wrote sizeable checks to charities for abused children, battered women, and the homeless. She replied to RSVP invitations, and she'd been inundated with mail of no consequence, which she trashed. When she was finished, she went into the kitchen to have breakfast. The food that had looked so tempting when Yvonne first laid it on the table before her had lost much of its appeal, and she ended up pushing it away. After making several phone calls, she started a new play. However hard she tried, it was difficult to concentrate. Her mind was occupied. Not only with her parents, but Ralph as well.

When she returned to New York unexpectedly, she went by Ralph's apartment to surprise him. Although she heard soft music coming through his apartment door, he did not answer his doorbell.

Rayanne looked through her purse for her key, but could not locate it. She rang the bell again and although Ralph still didn't answer, she could no longer hear the music.

Before Rayanne could get to her condo, Ralph called on her cell phone. He convinced her to come back to his apartment. She did because she'd missed him and was anxious to see him.

When Rayanne entered Ralph's apartment, his scent hung in the air. Ralph took Rayanne into his arms and kissed her passionately and she responded as a woman who was deeply in love with her man would respond. After they'd made love and Rayanne got up to go to the bathroom, she was about to walk out when something caught her eye. There was a nearly half-full bottle of perfume on the sink. It wasn't one of the fragrances that she wore.

Rayanne picked up the bottle and walked back out to Ralph's bedroom. "Who does this belong to?" she asked.

Ralph sat up in bed. "What is that?" he asked.

"Perfume, but it certainly isn't one of mine," Rayanne said suspiciously.

"Are you sure?" he asked, looking nervous.

"Yes, darling, I'm sure," she said sarcastically. "I like Chanel but it's not one that I wear."

"Well, I don't know. And you said it was in my bathroom?"

Rayanne blew air out of her mouth and rolled her eyes toward the ceiling. Then she began putting her clothes on.

"Baby, what are you doing? I don't know where the perfume came from. I've never seen it before," Ralph said, and Rayanne could see his mind racing. "Oh, I . . . ah . . . I remember now," he stuttered. "Bob, you remember my friend Bob, right? Well, he and his girl stopped over the other night and come to think of it, she did ask to use the bathroom. I bet that perfume belongs to her."

"Whatever," Rayanne said, and picked up her purse. She could see why any woman would be turned on by Ralph, his sexy smile and bedroom eyes. He certainly had turned her on the night she met him and he was still doing it, she thought. But hadn't they decided on an exclusive relationship?

"But where are you going? Why are you leaving, Rayanne?"

"Ralph, I am tired and I haven't been home yet. I'll call you later," she said, and left.

Rayanne reviewed her previous notes, organized, then reorganized them, jotted a few sentences, looked at them, then crossed them out. After several repeats, she put on her sneakers and walked around the block. A nice vigorous walk had always proved successful for her writer's block in the past.

When Rayanne returned to the condo, she sat at the desk and picked up the pen again, but still, the words didn't flow. She pushed the pen and pad aside, sat deep in her chair, and sighed. Her father had been released from the hospital two months ago and although he appeared to have recovered fully, there was something about the way he looked that Rayanne couldn't put out of her mind. She could hardly concentrate on anything else for thinking about her parents, her father in particular. She dialed their number.

"Hey, Mama," Rayanne said when her mother answered the phone.

Helen, knowing her daughter well enough to

know why she was calling, said softly, "Everything is fine here, honey. How are you?"

"I'm fine. Just checking on you all," Rayanne said, not wanting to let her mother know how worried she was, but her own voice betrayed her and before she realized it, she asked, "Is he all right?"

"Yes, he's all right."

Rayanne wanted to ask whether her father was still working as hard, but she refrained, trying to shut out the mental picture of him toiling from dawn to dusk, growing older and more worn day by day. "And, yes, your Daddy's still working hard," Helen said, answering her daughter's silent question.

"Daddy really should take it easy. Enjoy the grandchildren and just chill out."

"Raymond ain't gon' let nothing stop him," Helen said, and it was true. She knew her husband better than anyone and she knew that he liked being busy. Helen had always said that she didn't think Raymond would live long if he didn't have his work. He liked doing things that were meaningful.

"Daddy acts like he's on somebody's clock. Mama, I wish you would talk to him. He's killing himself and why? Y'all certainly don't need the money," Rayanne said, but she knew as her mother did that her father was set in his ways and once he made up his mind to do something, he rarely ever changed it.

"Honey, some of us have to do our own chores. We don't have someone to drive us around, or cook and pick up after us," Helen teased, but when Rayanne didn't respond, she said, "All joking aside, we're all concerned about your daddy, but you know how bullheaded he can be. And I can just see that buckle in your brow right now, so take it out."

Helen laughed. Rayanne laughed a little too. "I love your daddy too. He's the only man I ever loved, and I'll be the first to say that he does work too hard, but I ain't never tried to change him in all the years I've known him and I ain't gonna start now. I ain't got no right trying to do nothin' like that."

"But, Mama."

"Honey, I done talked to your daddy and he knows how I feel about all them long hours he's working, but how he wants to go about living his life is up to him. I want my man, but I want him happy."

"All right," Rayanne said. She knew she'd never be able to convince her mother otherwise. "You're wonderful, Mama."

"Sure I am. I'm your Mama, ain't I?"

"You most definitely are," Rayanne said, and after a moment asked, "You all right?"

"I'm fine," Helen replied, and Rayanne wondered. She knew her mother liked protecting them. "Everything's all right, thanks the Lord."

"I don't know why I can't shake this feeling of uneasiness." It was silly but she felt that as long as she was at home, nothing bad would happen, but the moment she stepped on the plane, leaving South Carolina, she began to worry and felt that each time the phone rang, it was bringing bad news. It was silly, very silly, but that was how she felt.

"You're a worrywart, that's why. You worry about everything. You'd worry or feel responsible if there was one of them earthquakes in Africa." Helen paused. "Things are gonna happen, but we can't live, looking for bad things around every corner. We gotta have a little faith, live life to the fullest, and trust in the Lord. No matter what happens, however bad it might be, God will give us the wisdom to know what to do and the strength to do it."

Rayanne agreed with all her mother had said, but an earthquake in Africa? She had to smile.

"Worrying ain't gonna do but one thing for you. It'll make an old lady out of you before your time, take it from me. Oh, did I tell you?" Helen said, changing the subject. "Maxine is planning to go back to school in the evenings, she said. Me and your daddy will help look after the children. By the way, when are you gonna settle down and give your daddy and me some grandchildren?"

"I don't know," Rayanne responded.

"You ain't getting any younger, you know," Helen teased.

"No kidding?" Rayanne came back, joking. "I'm just not ready yet."

"What about Ralph? Is he ready?" Helen pressed.

"He's been for some time now, Mama. He's waiting on me," she said, and suddenly an uneasy feeling came to rest around her shoulders again. Maybe it was simply because she was tired.

"Well, don't wait too long," Helen said, then asked, "How's that other daughter of mine?"

"Lila and I talked a couple of weeks ago," Rayanne replied, knowing that wouldn't go over well with her mother. If mama had it her way, Rayanne and Lila would be calling or seeing each other every day.

"Y'all live right there together. You oughta be talking more than that."

Rayanne and Lila didn't talk much because it was always Rayanne who initiated the calls, and even when she did, Lila was either too tired, too busy, or on her way out. Often times when Rayanne tried to get her but couldn't and left a message on her machine, Lila seldom bothered to return the call. *So what's the use?* Rayanne thought.

"You know Lila. She's got her own little world mapped out and she ain't gonna let nothin' bother it, but she's my daughter, your oldest sister, and I love her as you ought to. She just likes doing things her way."

It was more than that, but that was Lila's business, Rayanne thought, and the less she had to do with it, the better.

"I talked with Jeremy day before yesterday," Helen continued, "and I told Lila it's not a good idea for no thirteen-year-old to be staying in no apartment by hisself like that, so she's gonna make some other arrangements."

"I'll call and check on them," Rayanne said.

The following afternoon Rayanne had guests over for dinner, Ivory and Desmond, Dorian and Henry, and Ralph. Yvonne was on vacation and Rayanne prepared the meal, which consisted of a leafy salad, white potatoes, and steaks to grill, coleslaw, and baked beans. She'd even baked a couple of sweet potato pies for dessert. Rayanne was in the kitchen when Dorian appeared. "Hey, hey, hey," Rayanne said, swaying to the music that oozed into the kitchen from the terrace. "How's it going?"

"Things are good. You?"

"Everything's everything," Rayanne answered. "What are they doing out there?"

"They're talking stock options and golf at the club," Dorian said, and making quotes with her fingers, added, "Boring."

"Aaah," Rayanne said, and laughed.

She and Ivory had talked Dorian into going into a rehabilitation center and she'd been clean for six months now and she looked good and appeared happy again. They'd learned through Dorian's therapy that her parents were killed and she had felt such a sense of abandonment that she lived with the fear of being alone. She was still seeing Henry, but Rayanne and Ivory had stopped mentioning it long ago. Sometime people have to decide for themselves what is best for them.

"Where's Yvonne?" Dorian asked.

"She's on vacation," Rayanne said, busy tearing lettuce apart for the salad.

"You put all this stuff together yourself?"

"This is nothing," Rayanne said, dipped a piece of lettuce into a bowl of salad dressing, and stuck it into Dorian's mouth.

"Ummm, that is delicious." Dorian picked up a carrot stick, dipped it into the dressing, and took a bite of it. "This is so good. New dressing?"

"It's just a little something I threw together. A package of dressing mix, a dash of salt, pepper, Accent, a little mustard, blend it all together, and this is what I got. So, what have you been up to? You look great."

"I've been fine," Dorian said, and it was true. Ivory and Rayanne had nagged her to the point that she'd gotten the help she needed with her drug problem, and she looked so much better. "I've got a fashion show tomorrow night. You know, the fund-raiser for the Heart Assocation."

"Yeah. I'll be there," Rayanne popped a piece of cucumber into her mouth. "You look great, girl."

"I feel good," Dorian replied. "How are things

going with you? Are you still writing?" Rayanne admitted that the ideas were not coming as before, nothing she could sink her teeth into and get the juices flowing, she said, a frown on her face, which Dorian noticed. "You're just having writer's block, but that'll pass." What she didn't know was that Rayanne was more preoccupied with what might be going on back home than she was with her writing career, but she smiled and nodded yes.

Ivory joined the girls in the kitchen. "What are you two talking about?"

"And how are you too?" Rayanne said, and laughed.

"Girl, my body is here, but I left my head out there somewhere," Ivory mumbled because Dorian had stuck a piece of lettuce dipped with salad dressing into her mouth.

"Isn't this sensational?" Dorian asked.

"Ummm, yeah. Delicious. What is it?" Ivory asked.

"Just a little something I whipped up," Rayanne said, then checked the rolls in the oven, removed them, and set them on top of the stove. And, pointing to the top cabinet, she said, "Grab a dish from that cabinet, please." Ivory brought the dish over, slid the rolls from the sheet into it, and covered them with a towel. "Dorian has a fashion show tomorrow night," Rayanne said. "The one sponsored by the Heart Association."

"Oh yeah. That's right. What time?" Ivory asked, and tore off a piece of bread.

"Eight," Rayanne answered, removing a dish of coleslaw from the refrigerator.

"Who's gonna eat all this food?" Ivory asked, moving her hand in a sweeping gesture. "You've got enough here to feed an army." She picked up another piece from the salad bowl, and Rayanne looked at her.

"Ivory, you're munching all over the place. You pregnant?" Rayanne asked, a smile on her face.

"You'd like to be an aunt again, wouldn't you?" Ivory made fun of Rayanne. "Well, no. I ain't pregnant."

"I just asked because you seem to have quite an appetite, girlfriend." Rayanne continued with the food, but still watched Ivory as well.

"Gal, please," Ivory said just as Ralph poked his head through the door.

"Girls, what's going on in here?" he asked. "The steaks are ready and the party's outside."

"We're coming. Come, girls," Rayanne said, picking up a couple of bowls of food. "Grab a dish and take it out to the terrace."

The unfortunate thing was that by the time the food was moved out to the terrace and they began to eat, it started to rain.

Chapter 21

Rayanne met Ralph in the lobby of the building on Wall Street where he worked. When he approached her, long gone was his tailored suit and shirt and tie that transformed him from an average guy to Corporate America. He'd changed into a pair of white slacks, a tan pullover, and a pair of white sneakers. Rayanne was comfortably dressed in a pair of yellow slacks, a sleeveless yellow blouse, and white sneakers, and she wore her hair in a ponytail. They first had a glass of iced tea at an outdoor restaurant, and then they took a taxi to the dock where they boarded a small boat and they ate dinner while circling the city. They watched the lights onshore as they twinkled and almost vanished as the boat moved farther away from shore.

It was a lovely summer night and the breeze that came off the water was cool and pleasant. Ralph and Rayanne stood close to each other and watched the moonlight as it cast a silvery path across the water. They strolled around on the boat, listening to soft music played by the band that was set up on the stern. When they docked, they ran off the boat, hand in hand, and came upon an ice-cream shop. Ralph chose chocolate chip, Rayanne had buttered pecan.

"Yours looks delicious," she said.

"So does yours."

"If you give me a lick of yours, I'll give you a lick of mine," she said, and when she looked up at him, he was smiling wickedly, as he handed the cashier a bill to cover their purchase.

"That was a dangerous statement," he said.

"You know what I meant," she said, laughed, and punched him gently in the ribs.

"Now she's trying to kill me." He was holding his chest pretending to be in pain. He put his arm around her shoulders and they walked along the sidewalk. They'd been rushing so much from the time they met that neither had inquired about the kind of day the other had. Rayanne asked.

"It was crazy and busy," he replied, remembering how hectic his day was before they met. "And yours?"

"Not bad," she said, looking up at him as they continued their walk, hand in hand, enjoying the evening breezes. "You want to talk about it?" she asked, noticing his perplexed look.

"Maybe later."

"You sure?"

"I'm sure."

After a while, Rayanne looked at Ralph and asked, "Are you tired?"

"No. Why do you ask?" His look grew more perplexed.

"I'd like to go over to Broadway and walk around a little, but if you're not up to it, we don't have to."

"No, I'm fine."

"Interested?"

"Sure," he said.

"Ralph, really, we don't have to if you don't want," she teased.

"What do you mean? I said I'm fine. I know I'm a little older than you but . . ." he began.

"A little older?" Rayanne continued to tease. "A little older?"

"All right. So I'm ten years older, but I'm not ready for a rocking chair," he said, sounding annoyed.

Rayanne looked at Ralph. He looked tired and she was already sorry she'd teased him. "Honey, I was only teasing. I didn't offend you, did I?" She stopped and held his hand tightly so that they faced each other. "Are you upset?" He didn't respond. "Ralph, I was only kidding," she said. He looked at her, but he still didn't respond. "Ralph, I'm sorry. I had no idea you were so sensitive about your age." He freed his hand and turned to walk away, but Rayanne rushed after him, caught his arm, and turned him around to face her again. "Ralph," she said, looking very serious.

"Gotcha," he said, pointing a finger at her and laughing out loud.

"What?" she said.

"I said gotcha," he repeated, threw his head back, and laughed.

Rayanne smiled then, shook her head, and punched him in the arm really hard this time. "I got you that time, didn't I?" He was still laughing at her. "Honey, I'm approaching middle age but I don't have a problem with that. Why? Because I'm all man. Maybe I won't be so quick to say that in thirty years, but right now I'm pretty confident. My health is good, I have a great job, and I've got a young beautiful woman by my side. I've got nothing to frown about. Hell, life can't get much better than this," he said, looking at her. He laughed again, caught her hand, and they resumed walking and before heading to her condo, they browsed in some of the twenty-four-hour shops on Broadway. Then Ralph offered to get a taxi.

"Why don't we get the bus?" Rayanne said.

"All right," Ralph said, looked back, and saw the bus coming up behind them. "If you want to catch the next one, we've got about a minute to cross the street and get to the corner because it's coming," he said, and he started to run. Rayanne had never mentioned that she'd run track while in high school. Ralph had a head start of about a couple of yards, but Rayanne sprinted and caught up with him. She cut across in front of him, reached back, and caught his hand, and they ran across the street between traffic, with horns honking and wheels screeching. "Hey, you," Ralph yelled, "we've got to be careful. Haven't you heard about these crazy New York drivers? You're going to get us both killed."

"Shut your mouth and run," she said, holding his hand and laughing. "Come on, you're such a baby."

"Maybe, but I'm your baby," he said, almost out of breath. They reached the corner ahead of the bus and Ralph was breathing heavily when they boarded and found seats.

"Let's ride to the end of the line and back," Rayanne suggested.

"All right," he said, and Rayanne snuggled up next to him, resting her head on his shoulder and closing her eyes. He looked down into her face. "Happy?"

She opened her eyes, looked at him, and answered, "Very."

"Me too," he whispered. "I love you."

"Me too," she said.

"You too what?" he teased.

"Me too, love you," she answered, and linked her arm through his.

After a moment Ralph said, a puzzled look on his face, "Where did you learn to run like that?"

Rayanne laughed, nestling closer to him as they rode in silence, watching the city unfold before their eyes.

They arrived at the condo, and they collapsed on the couch. After a while Rayanne attempted to get up to check her messages, but Ralph pinned her down with his arms. She was grateful he was no longer abusing drugs anymore and that he'd loved her enough to kick the habit. He was no longer nervous or appeared anxious as he did in the past. She'd never loved him as much as she did at that moment. When Ralph and Rayanne made love that night, it was intense, filled with passion, and unlike any other time before.

After Ralph left in the morning, Rayanne listened to her messages. Ivory called to say she'd be out of town a few days, and the other two were from her mother. Her father had been hospitalized again, he'd suffered another heart attack, and at 2:15 that afternoon, Rayanne was on her way back home, thoughts and guilt consuming her. She wished she'd checked her messages last night.

This attack was far more damaging than the first, and Raymond looked much older than when Rayanne had last seen him. He stayed in the hospital ten days this time, and during that trip, Rayanne took time to reflect. She took long drives in the country, she worked with her mother in the yard, and she gave a lot of thought to what she wanted to do with the rest of her life.

Rayanne had been blessed beyond her wildest dreams. She had accomplished everything she had aspired to and more, so much more. God had bestowed many wonderful blessings on her. She looked to God for guidance throughout her life and she would continue to look to Him for answers. Rayanne had found that even when she was having the best of times, her thoughts were centered on her parents and their well-being. She considered all the possibilities and when she made her mind up, the decision wasn't a difficult one. It became crystal clear to her one day as she sat alone on her front porch, and two weeks after her father was released from the hospital, Rayanne returned to New York.

Rayanne spent several months lining up some projects as well as finalizing some business deals. Raytiff was expanding. They were handling an enormous amount of business and the office manager was doing a good job of keeping the office running smoothly as well as keeping Rayanne and Tiffany abreast of all aspects of the operation. Ivory and Dorian were out of town so often that they didn't see each other very often anyway, though they never allowed too much time to pass without getting together and catching up. It wasn't as easy selling her most recent decision to Ralph, but in the end he said he understood. Hadn't he always been supportive and understanding of whatever it was that she had to do? After all, people were involved in long-distance relationships all the time and some of them worked out very well. In any event at the end of January and after some tearful good-byes and one final carriage ride along Central Park, Rayanne packed up and moved back to South Carolina.